JOHAN BORGEN : THE SCAPEGOAT

Some other books from Norvik Press

Sigbjørn Obstfelder: *A Priest's Diary* (translated by James McFarlane)
Hjalmar Söderberg: *Short stories* (translated by Carl Lofmark)
Annegret Heitmann (ed.): *No Man's Land. An Anthology of Modern Danish Women's Literature*
P C Jersild: *A Living Soul* (translated by Rika Lesser)
Sara Lidman: *Naboth's Stone* (translated by Joan Tate)
Selma Lagerlöf: *The Löwensköld Ring* (translated by Linda Schenck)
Villy Sørensen: *Harmless Tales* (translated by Paula Hostrup-Jessen)
Camilla Collett: *The District Governor's Daughters* (translated by Kirsten Seaver)
Jens Bjørneboe: *The Sharks* (translated by Esther Greenleaf Mürer)
Jørgen-Frantz Jacobsen: *Barbara* (translated by George Johnston)
Janet Garton & Henning Sehmsdorf (eds. and trans.): *New Norwegian Plays* (by Peder W. Cappelen, Edvard Hoem, Cecilie Løveid and Bjørg Vik)
Gunilla Anderman (ed.): *New Swedish Plays* (by Ingmar Bergman, Stig Larsson, Lars Norén and Agneta Pleijel)

The logo of Norvik Press is based on a drawing by Egil Bakka (University of Bergen) of a Viking ornament in gold, paper thin, with impressed figures (size 16x21mm). It was found in 1897 at Hauge, Klepp, Rogaland, and is now in the collection of the Historisk museum, University of Bergen (inv.no. 5392). It depicts a love scene, possibly (according to Magnus Olsen) between the fertility god Freyr and the maiden Gerðr; the large penannular brooch of the man's cloak dates the work as being most likely 10th century.

Cover illustration: *Protection/Bars* by Hilde Mæhlum.

Johan Borgen

THE SCAPEGOAT

TRANSLATED BY ELIZABETH ROKKAN

Norvik Press
1993

About the translator:

Elizabeth Rokkan was born in Wales and graduated from the University College of Wales, Aberystwyth, moving to Norway after her marriage. She was until recently Senior Lecturer in the English Department of the University of Bergen. She has translated Norwegian short stories, poetry, and the novels of Cora Sandel and Tarjei Vesaas: these have included Sandel's *Alberta* trilogy and Vesaas's *The House in the Dark* — his allegory of the Norwegian experience of the Second World War — as well as the Nordic Prizewinning novel *The Ice Palace*, recently re-issued in Britain and the United States.

Original title: *Jeg*. First published 1959.
© Gyldendal Norsk Forlag, Oslo.
This translation © Elizabeth Rokkan 1993.
All Rights Reserved

British Library Cataloguing in Publication Data
Borgen, Johan
   The Scapegoat
   I. Title. II. Rokkan, Elizabeth.
   839.82374 [F]
ISBN 1-870041-21-6

First published in 1993 by Norvik Press, University of East Anglia,
   Norwich, NR4 7TJ, England
Managing Editors: James McFarlane and Janet Garton

Norvik Press has been established with financial support from the University of East Anglia, the Danish Ministry for Cultural Affairs, The Norwegian Cultural Department, and the Swedish Institute. Publication of this book has been aided by a grant from the Norwegian Ministry of Culture.

Printed in Great Britain by Biddles Ltd, Guildford, Surrey.

I

1

A bird flies, dark above slate-grey water. I come out of the house. I see myself from where I am standing at the edge of the forest. The first ray of sun strikes the veranda door through which I have just come. As for myself, I am standing in dew-wet shade.

This has occurred before, the fact that I am divided. It always occurs when something is about to happen. Which means that something is not simply going to happen around me or in me, but *to* me. You can't be alone in such a situation, because it has to happen to the one, while the other must know about it and explain it to both of us.

And this is a day for flight. I know this after weeks in a forest which is breaking into leaf. There are still snow patches in soft hollows of moss, and grey sheets of snow are spread on the northern slopes. There the firs stand dark and dense. But down by the lake, in a semi-circle round the house, the birches are green, their tops full of gaiety. It's an invitation to lethargy, to lazy, inconsequential reflection.

That is why I lock the door and turn my back on the house and watch myself walk along the path that leads away from the lake and climbs up the hill on the shady side. Only when I am up at the place where the trees are slender and small do I meet the sun again and know that the house down there behind me is lying bathed in the cool gold of morning. Down there I stand and say, 'Will he turn back?' I watch myself pause to get my breath, but know that this business of getting one's breath is a fraud, an excuse to turn round.

And I ask again from down there whether he will turn back.

'If he does he is lost.'

If he does I shall have to experience yet again that resigned shrug of the shoulders. Afterwards he will set off home, lightfooted along the path. As before, as so many times before. I say, 'Is he really so incapable of taking a decision?' He is still standing there. On his back he has a small knapsack. It contains just enough of the few things he considers necessary, suitable for emptying into the cupboard in a casual hotel room. Not casual, however. I know that if he does go, he will look for the little hotel opposite the park with the bronze child and the many fountains. He will not know exactly why he goes there, but I shall know.

First he will find the motor cycle in the old stable on the other side of the yard at the Farm. And the farm is called the Farm; it has no other name. They will see him from the windows; perhaps the old man will come out, perhaps not. Even the smallest question from the old man can have fatal consequences for his decision. For example, the old man may say, 'Well, so you're going on your travels?' Then he will reply, 'No, not today', put the cycle back, and go home.

But if he turns round now, up there in the golden halo that the sun is creating around him and the last red pine trunks? Then he is lost. I stand with my heart hammering in my chest and order him to go. But not too sternly — with gentle words in my thoughts. *If* he decides, it will be an instant decision as far as he is aware; not because he wishes it. Because that's the problem: he does not wish to go further, he does not wish to wish. A squirrel leaps between low branches right beside him. He has noticed it, it's coming towards him. It may give him the excuse to turn round, but he stands his ground, he does not turn round. On the contrary, what is he doing? That's astonishing! He's kneeling. He's kneeling on both knees with his knapsack on his back — a curious whim. For we are not in the habit of praying.

Then he gets to his feet quickly and walks on. He vanishes on the instant.

I go and touch the wall of the cabin, feeling its comfortable timber. The scent of wood in a mounting sun lies like a girdle round the house. Longing to be back here, I walk to the fragile jetty with the boat rocking to and fro on its rope with its inexpressibly peaceful movement between the jetty and the post; to the fishing net which is standing between the dead aspen and a forked stick. Once a bird got caught in the net, a robin ...

The motor cycle roars along the road to town. A cloud of dust rises behind it and turns into fog, a thick pall of greasy exhaust hovering above the meadows. This is evil. The many miles to town are not peaceful. Peace is behind us now, gone. Everything standing still — houses, trees — looks petrified in the face of this inexorable movement.

A child runs across the road. He knocks it down ...
Did a child run across the road? Did I knock it down?
No, not this time. The child got away. It was a narrow escape. But the next time?
A child runs across the road. Well, that one got away too; it was not to be that child.

His speed stays the same because the road demands it. It sucks into and beneath the front wheel. The rear wheel spits out the surface like an evil fog above all the fields. Houses, trees, people in the fields — they all petrify in the face of this speed, which is evil. Then a child runs across the road. His brakes screech; he saw it in time and slowed down. But the child changed its mind as well; it stood still, hesitating. Both of them hesitate. Then he accelerates again. But the child also changed its mind when he slowed down. And now the child runs. The man and the child are guided by the same thoughts; they have hesitated, they have made a decision. The child runs as he accelerates. There is a thump. There is no longer a child in the road, but bloody clothes, guts in greasy dust, a rag doll with a head screwed on, an astonishingly unhurt head. A scream rings out briefly from the fence. That's true. Someone was sitting there a short while ago; a second ago a grandmotherly figure sat knitting in a chair on the lawn in front of the house. The figure was knitting in the sunshine, the light reflected in her glasses. Now she is on her feet, it was she who screamed — a brief, piercing scream. Now the garment she was knitting is flapping in the wind, hanging on the back of the chair.

What now? Didn't the child get away? A doll is lying in the road, with real guts that are bleeding in the dust. The grandmother is not screaming. She, too, has become one of the petrified objects; only the knitting is flapping in the wind, alive, a child's garment which is alive, but it lacks an arm, as if it had been run over. The world is changed in some way. There is no longer a child running across the road. A child is lying in the road. A motor cycle is resting crookedly against the edge of the ditch. And there are many people. Everything is changed.

The world is changed. It had been a cheerful morning — or hadn't it? Now the sun is black with light. He had been driving; he was on his way to town. A child had appeared, it wanted to cross the road, it hesitated, what happened? Everything is changed. It is a different place; he is in a cold, naked room without shadows. But he only sees a sleeveless garment flapping in the wind. A man in brown clothes is sitting at a table.
Your name? Address? Driving licence number?
He sees only a garment flapping in the wind. The world is changed, into a completely different world.
Well, let's try again.
'Your name?'
'My name was ...'
'Why do you say *was*?'
A pause. The garment is flapping somewhere on the back of a chair.
You were on your way to — ?
You were on your way from — ?
You were driving at what speed? There are people who say ...
'A child crossed the road.'
'Thank you, we know that. A little girl. She's dead.'
Someone said *dead*. Someone is trying to re-experience it, or merely experience it. He cannot experience anything, not anything. He has never ... or has he? It had something to do with a road, a child.
'It had something to do with a road, a child.'
'It *had* something to do with a child. She is dead. Killed.'

'Did you say killed?'

'So: your name? We'll start again. You say it *was* — ?'

Now the world is changed. Through all the days and the long nights after this, the world will be different, without limits, without comfort.

Perhaps it's only a dream, a fantasy?

That's not important now. Something has happened. Something has happened, and everything is being played backwards. All his thoughts come now, they come afterwards.

What if you hadn't accelerated?

What if you had waited for the child?

Or if you had not waited?

What if you had passed five minutes earlier?

Or later?

What if the child had not been that child but another child, a child who had waited? Or a child who had just run across the road while there was still time, to play with the neighbour's child over the way?

Or what if there had been no child?

What if you had not been there at all, or were not you?

What if there had been no parents staring with empty eyes from the witness box?

No, not at you. They're not staring at you, just staring.

No grandmother with a half-knitted blue sweater — now it's hanging over the back of a chair on the same lawn in front of the house. Which house? The house from which the child came to run across to the neighbour's house. What if there had been no house? What if there had been no child, for this child to cross over to play with? What if there had been no children in the whole world and no myself, or another person driving past, or rather, no other person ...

'No guilt can be ascribed to the driver of the motor cycle.'

No guilt, no guilt in the long nights, the long days, dark as the nights. No guilt? You can go, sir! You can go, mate! I can go!

He went. He walked and walked. He was free as the air, without guilt, branded innocent, more so than people who had not driven along that road that day when she ran across it. Simply authorized innocent, guiltless as a summer sky an hour or two after dawn, when it happened. The man is guiltless, the only guiltless man in the world. Free, free. The only free person in a world of bondage. — Your name as a free man? — Residence? — Position? — You don't understand? — What your name is, where you live and how you make your living? A pure formality as long as a man is free. Are you not free? Isn't your name free? We don't understand. Oh, I see — *you* don't understand. Perhaps not. But such things happen. That's how it is. Such things happen. An accident. One after another here and all over the world. All sorts of things happen. Nothing remains the same from one moment to the next. You, for instance, were not a free man, now you are free ... You haven't the same name? You're not the same person? You refuse to be the person who suffered ... suffered ... an accident? Everyone agrees that it was an accident. Even the grandmother who was sitting on a chair on the lawn in front of the house behind the fence — she says it was purely an accident. You say the knitting is still hanging there? We know nothing about that. That the house is still standing there, but that it's a different house? That the road is different, the grass on the lawn, the road and the sun and the sky? No, begging your pardon, *we* don't understand. We are the authorities, and we say it's the same road and the same house. We don't know anything about any knitting ... You must on no account come and tell us that you're not free. You have been acquitted, that's more than being free; somebody who is acquitted cannot possibly be guilty. You may go wherever you like. If you wish to go up that street, then go up it; if, on the contrary, it occurs to you to go down the street, in the direction of the post office — that's the big red building with the pointed tower — well, you can go there. You can go wherever you like. Do you understand what we are saying? You can go wherever you like. We are the authorities — this is what we say ... You say you can't go? You say you won't go? Extraordinary! Do you set yourself up against the authorities? You know better? How well do you know that, then? The authorities say you are not guilty.

And now I whisper from a long way off, as firmly as I can. You are not guilty. Perhaps you ought never to have started on that short journey, which turned into that long journey because each yard you covered between us amounted to many miles. But you did it. You did not hesitate on the crest of the hill, when you were standing as if spun about with sunshine. You went, and what happened was that I sent my anxiety, my accident-creating fantasy, after you. You did not kill. They say you killed no one, so you did not kill. Life is not a question of what might have been, but of what is; not of what might have happened, not of your guilty mind, life is a question of deeds. And I say that what happened was that I had filled you with my fantasies, pregnant with misfortune, which served to protect you against departure, which said: You are still living between the house and the jetty with the fishing net hanging up, where a robin got caught; in the forest with the solemn fir trees, where you whistled contentedly on the doorstep when you threw out the water into the summer night at bedtime. It was the force of my imaginative foreboding which told you that this was best, not action and heroics. But there was a resolve in you, an unfortunate urge to take decisions. It grew by the hour, even though I undermined it a little. And now I tell you that you have not killed any child!

If I tell you that for *my* sake you must continue this resolve that I fought against with my warnings? When I combine my voice with that of authority, an authority you have always feared more than anything, because you are a respectable citizen ... can't you hear me, even though the distance is great? We're shouting to you that you're not guilty, yes, you're free. What does it matter that I've warned you, however earnestly, about these shocking things? It's facts that count, after all, only facts, not warnings and predictions, not belief or doubt. It's a question of one thing: guilty or not — of the one *and* the other. Can't you learn that? It's so simple. Everyone lives accordingly, and prospers. They prosper increasingly, only look about you.

You say a garment is hanging over the back of a chair. You say it's blue, that one arm is missing, you say she stood up with an appalled expression. You say she screamed. Is that all you have to plead in defence of your guilt?

But since they say that in fact that's all you did see, this garment, this grandmother, perhaps you imagined a child, imagined a possibility; because of all that fear I had filled you with in order to hold you back in a unity I thought was us, was you, therefore was our Self. Since I tell you all this and you have believed me up to now, believed my worst suspicions, can't you then believe, can't you accept that what they say is true: that you're free and blameless from this day forward?

There we are! That's better! From the sun-baked wall of the cabin I am watching myself now. He is striding along the street in town, quite cheerful and quite self-confident, his head held high. His steps are firm.

He paused on the steps of the post office, a letter in his hand. Then he changed his mind, tore it in half and threw it into the litter bin beside the gate to the park, instead of putting it in the post-box. Now he's whistling.

Hooray, now things are much better! He looks about him, feeling the need of company. That's right! Nothing like companionship when you're upset. A fellow human being is a simple thing, a human being simply. A fellow human being is what he appears to be: that's how he is, a sum total of voice, thoughts, movements and whims. Everyone can do that sort of calculation. A fellow human being is a matter of simple addition.

Would you believe it, he's greeting someone too! His fellow human being is a woman, quite a lady in fact. He must know her already, because she stops, she smiles, he takes her arm. They have plans for the night already. For look, the sun is setting behind the post office tower. A fellow human being is a simple matter, a person. And a woman into the bargain. She is a woman, that makes it even simpler. I know he's almost home and dry already. I know you're almost home and dry. Perhaps there's a slight pang in my heart at this moment. I wander out on to the doorstep towards nightfall and read the signs: the light above the birches, the dark bird grazing the tips of the fir trees on the other side of the lake. But it's going well, after all. I know I'm almost home and dry, or I'm at any rate on my way. It did help a bit to talk urgently across that great distance, about this freedom that we have, you, I. Everyone possesses it after all. And all the others are straightforward. So why should you ...?

2

Can my concern be called fraternal? I don't think so. Not even comradely, merely egotistical on behalf of his stay-at-home self. So you needn't hesitate to call me a pimp. For he has had five women during these four days and it has warmed my heart, my part of my heart. Never mind the fact that his pleasure was mingled with — no, not guilt. He is not self-reproachful on that account. It's a yearning, a homesickness. It's a yearning for the woman who is not there when somebody else is in his bed.

Now what? He went too far. On the third day he went too far. He is naive after all. He believes that the big city obliges you to commit vice. He went too far between the third and fourth woman and enjoyed the last two in feverish drunkenness; with the last of them he was almost unconscious.

At such moments I lose my hold on him when I call from the timber wall of the house in the forest. He cuts the connection.

On purpose? I don't know. He keeps in touch through the first bottle; that's when he is so strongly in contact that my whole self vibrates. In the course of the second he suddenly throws it off, as one casts off a mooring.

Afterwards he sails along on his own. The journey home goes painfully, in fits and starts. I'm not saying I'm glad about that; and if I said, 'That'll do him good', it would be a lie. He suffers. But it repeats itself. It repeats itself.

He woke up without arms or legs. He was only a head, a

shattered head. As yet it lacked thoughts, being merely filled with waves of pain. But wait ...

He moved. Not his arms or legs — they were not there — but the skin of his body. A shiver went through it, like the skin of a horse when it shakes off horse flies nervously. Another twitch. The shoulders as well. Flies were wading persistently in the glue of his forehead, but he had no hand with which to wave them away. He tried to chase them off with his thoughts, but they did not surface, at least not the kinds of thoughts that could chase flies away. He twisted his head round cautiously, and the flies were so tired that some of them let themselves be killed against the pillow. The others crawled on, more joined them, and a few found their way towards the base of his nose and followed the delicious stream of the line of sweat towards the corners of his mouth, where they settled greedily. If only he had a hand. He glanced downwards with difficulty from under his swollen eyelids and surveyed his hands, each in turn. Strange, he thought feebly, that those hands couldn't help him — as if they were tied. All he could do was let his flickering memories find a way in. They resembled all other memories of debasement, without grandeur or singularity. His lips worked on a word, 'disgraceful', but they were glued together, his tongue was glued fast. The thought that was supposed to chase the flies away thought, 'disgraceful'. Not that it helped.

Then he knew he was in the hotel behind the park with the bronze child. It gave him such disquieting assurance that he immediately started preparing to leave.

It all took time, especially the buttons and laces. His shoes stood abused, their toes bent upwards, their laces in knots. It took him almost an hour to get them in order. But he did not swear, and he did not think while he was working on them. That's how things were. Such laces had their own personality; they might get so bad-tempered that they refused to obey you.

His feet refused to obey him on the staircase, too. But he did not curse them and call them bloody feet. He looked at them. Imploringly he looked at the plunging step on which his feet were standing, refusing to obey him. He treated them gently, one at a time, got them down the stairs, then diagonally across the floor of the lobby, where he placed his key on the desk like a sacrifice to a god. But the god behind the desk was merciful, and took no notice. He took so little notice of him that he thought, perhaps I'm not here?

And at that instant he knew, both question and answer.

Where?

The hotel.

I?

He raised his eyes to this god, who was a man with dark hair and a big nose; the lower of the two was the most visible thing about him. No chin, no mouth in this godlike position, bending forwards. He thought, he can't see me. I can creep away quietly and cease to exist where he's concerned.

He tripped over the mat at the revolving door, but the god behind him ignored him. I really am a nobody. As nobody he went out through the revolving door and struggled helplessly against the sunshine; it was everywhere. He had only one thought: if there was any shade perhaps he could find it. There was a dark opening: the entrance to the Public Hall beside the post office. He dived in, as if into water. A cool wooden bench was beneath him. Everything was cool, cellar-cool. On the rostrum stood a man with an old-fashioned lorgnette on a cord. He was talking about crime and the youth services and human caring.

'Murderers in this country,' he was saying, 'are entirely unprotected. Consider the case of Theodore, which the newspapers made known throughout the nation. A young man with excellent references from his Sunday School kills his prospective father-in-law with a shot from a sawn-off shot-gun. Unfortunate young man. What kind of childhood has he suffered? His foster-parents in the neighbouring valley gave him porridge several times a week, and Theodore cannot stand porridge. And as regards the shot-gun, it had been given him at his confirmation, and he had sawn off the barrel in order to shoot crows with it, out of consideration for the crows. That is how Theodore saw it; he is so fond of animals. He cannot give any information as to why he visited his father-in-law with the shot-gun. "I was in a kind of daze," he said. "I didn't know I had the shot-gun in my hand. I didn't know that I shot with it." And this is of some importance. When this unfortunate boy explained earlier that he took down the shot-gun from the wall in order to shoot his fiancée's father with it, he was under duress. "I can't remember saying anything like that," he said. Besides, the police told him he should say it. "I was in a kind of daze," he said. Besides, nobody knows what insults Theodore has had to suffer through the years, because his life style did not accord with the victim's taste; perpetual nagging that the boy ought to find himself something to do. His fiancée's attitude also became distorted in this way, her mind poisoned. She was fond of the boy as he was. He had never done her any harm to speak of. Neither was she particularly worried about the future, as her parents were. Her remark to the neighbouring housewife is typical of her cheerful and optimistic disposition. She was quoted as saying, "Why should my Theodore have something to do, when everyone else does so much?"

'To speak of intent in this connection, even of premeditation ...' The speaker raised his eyes and focused them on the audience, as if accusing anyone who might consider doing such a thing. He continued, more mildly:

'There are those who call for judgement. Perhaps that's only natural in their initial indignation. But who is to be judged? I do not speak of the murdered man. He was given his judgement. I speak of society, of the porridge if you like. But also of this endless nagging of our poor young people, who are living under the threat of appalling destruction by the atomic bomb. Will they survive into maturity, so that they in their turn can insult the young with all kinds of reproaches? Nobody can answer the nagging question: shall I be alive tomorrow, the day after tomorrow, next year?

'Theodore did not know. He does not know today. He was in a kind of daze, he said. Was that so strange? All young people today are in a daze. One day they stand with a shot-gun in their hands, they have sawn off the barrel, they don't know whether they have sawn it off themselves or whether it was sawn off at all, or whether what they are holding is a shot-gun. They are in a daze. An innocent daze, if you ask me! "Is it my fault that I was born?" asked Theodore of the prison chaplain. This question carries the message of a deep, brooding mind in distress. In great distress. In distress of the soul. I do not hesitate to say so. His classmates from the children's home witnessed in court that Theodore had a brooding nature, that he interfered when his comrades — in their youthful ignorance — tore the legs off dogs and cats. When the others amused themselves in this possibly rather violent fashion, Theodore fell into deep thought and considered that it was not right to act thus against defenceless animals. It is not surprising that he became less popular in his circle of friends. Boys are like that. And Theodore had, not just a thoughtful nature, but also the courage to express his convinced opinion about his comrades' actions. And all the time the porridge lay in his mind, a nagging memory, a cold hand of hostility and violence against that sensitive character.

'Nor is he strong, Theodore. He has a disability which has weighed on him heavily, say the experts. He has a slight squint in one eye. It may seem a small thing. But try it yourselves, all of you sitting here, active and healthy and perhaps censorious. Try squinting with your right eye as Theodore has done all his life, for eighteen endless years. Try it, I say. And then eat porridge at the same time! I imagine that anyone might find himself with a sawn-off shot-gun in his hand. And if you already have *that*, the distance to taking action is short, especially if you have a father-in-law ...'

By now it was obvious that the speaker had a good grip on his audience. Several of them nodded, and 'yes, yes' could be heard in low voices from the rows of benches.

'Perhaps Theodore was not like other children,' continued the speaker. 'On the other hand who is? Who is like others? Theodore was unique. Young people today are all unique. But what does society do about it? Society does nothing about young people who are unique. Is it then so strange that they shoot people? One of the experts, a psychiatrist whose name is known far beyond our country's borders, stated in court that Theodore is not merely a highly-gifted boy, but in addition a sub-normal boy. And who is one to believe if not the experts?

'It has been mentioned that Theodore told a friend that his father-in-law would end up a corpse. And people wish to regard this as an expression of evil intent towards the victim. But when are we going to accustom ourselves to accepting that the youth of today express themselves in a fashion different from what was usual fifty years ago? The statement was made in youthful elation, in a manifestation of good humour. For Theodore is humorous; the experts say so. He also has a very melancholy nature, they say. By "ending up a corpse" he only meant that he was not very pleased with his prospective father-in-law's attitude towards Theodore and his patterns of personal behaviour, his work habits, so to say. When are people in this country going to understand that what young people need above everything else is a leisure programme? We must set up institutes throughout the country for this purpose. I will go so far as to say that until we have organized a thoroughgoing programme for the occupation of young people in their leisure time, we shall continue to live in danger of our lives. What else can we expect? Our energetic youth must find something with which to occupy themselves. Leisure is the most important field of work in the future.'

The audience rose slowly from their seats. The speaker left the rostrum. This man was a college lecturer and a great friend of mankind. The poster said so. The audience formed groups in the deserted hall. They felt less certain of themselves now that the lecturer had gone. A grey-bearded man said to his group, 'That fellow Theodore ought to be hanged.' Another said, 'Is that the result?' 'The result of what?' The second speaker was a dark man with piercing eyes. 'Of what?' repeated the grey-beard angrily. 'Of the lecture, of all this education?' 'He ought to be hanged. First whipped, then hanged.' The two men faced each other, their eyes flashing. The group became larger.

He pushed forward towards the speakers listlessly. A young woman had come up close beside him. 'He's right,' she said. 'Who's right?' asked the man with the piercing eyes. 'He's right. A fellow like that ought to be whipped and beheaded.' But her irony made no impression on the pugnacious grey-beard. By now many eyes were flashing.

He stood close to the young woman, feeling solaced by this merciless desire to punish. He purposely misunderstood her irony and heard himself say, 'She's right.' And again the dark-haired man with the piercing eyes came forward. 'You mean that the law of retribution should prevail? And then retribution upon retribution — total war ...?' The dark man's face was ablaze. 'Say what you mean, since you have an opinion. You believe in punishment? You look about you at our society and believe in punishment?'

He heard himself say, 'I think it's good for us to be punished.'

But the other attacked him. Even the greybeard was against him now, and the young woman. He was asked whether he was in favour of punishment for the sake of the punished? He heard himself answer, 'We have it in us. A will to misfortune. It's good for us to expect punishment on account of our unfortunate will.'

Then they all attacked him, even those who were in favour of punishment. A woman said, 'He's crazy. He's a religious fanatic.' But the young woman who had been standing close to him pulled him gently by the sleeve of his jacket. There was an archway beside the door and she drew him towards it. 'Don't tease them,' she whispered. 'They're beside themselves with their liberalism.'

Afterwards he sat with the young woman in a bar. She drank a strong cocktail in order to calm down. He brought himself back to life by means of the old cure: long, healthy drinks with vitamins and scarcely any poison, until he had nevertheless taken enough alcohol to regain his composure. 'It's the vitamins,' he told her. 'When you've used up or destroyed all your vitamins with alcohol you have to replace them.' 'With alcohol?' she answered, smiling. He protested. 'No, with new vitamins in a form that's easily available.' She said, 'You must be more careful in this town. No, no, I know you don't come from here, or you haven't been here for some time. You don't get that kind of tan from sunbathing in town, only from being out of doors without sunbathing. You mustn't say things like that about people; that's what they say in the chapels out in the country. You can't tell enlightened people that they're hankering for punishment. That's Old Testament, perhaps Christian, I wouldn't know. These people are members of a humanist society, disagreeing amongst themselves on just about everything, except that human beings are free and ought to be even more free. They believe in reason.'

'And you?'

'That doesn't matter. Though I do believe in reason.' They drank with silent concentration. The conversation came in spurts, with brief questions and brief answers. Like this:

'You don't seem to find it in the least surprising that I, a virtuous young woman, should go off with you to a bar and discuss an unpleasant scene?'

'I find scarcely anything surprising. That least of all.'

'Maybe you're used to women ...'

'Spare me, spare us both. Here we are. Isn't that enough? You with your freedom — I don't suppose you believe in destiny?'

'And you, without freedom, you do?'

'Not unconditionally, not always. You didn't answer my question.'

'I don't believe in destiny.'

'The exact opposite, then? In free will?'

'What do you mean by free?'

'Free.'

'Then I believe in a will that's almost free.'

'And what about the will itself — do you believe in that? I mean, the will to be free.'

'I certainly believe in the will to be free.'

'But do you believe in the will itself to have a free will?'

'You mean the wish?'

'If you like. Do you believe in that? — You don't answer?'

'I'm thinking. I drink a little and think. I'm thinking, among other things, that if I had not drunk a couple of cocktails it would have been easy to answer your question.'

'Do you believe in the power of the wish itself?'

Again she thought for a little. 'That a person's wish — unspoken — can affect another person's will?'

'Precisely. To put it even more precisely: that a person's burning wish, unspoken and unexpressed in any other way — by look, touch, trick of the mind or whatever — that it has an equal power all the same, a power to influence minds solely because the wish is fostered; that the wish, to put it briefly, is an independent phenomenon capable of reshaping, influencing, even at a distance, even at a very great distance.'

She thought for a little and said, 'I could reduce your chatter to the most commonplace banality. I could make it contemptible, throw suspicion on it.'

'But you don't.'

'I'm trying to avoid it.'

They sat, silent, almost hostile. Then he said, and there was a painful passion in his voice that made her alter her decision to put an end to this absurd, objectionable meeting:

'For example, it is my constant wish to avoid a certain kind of banality in the situation that has arisen between us.'

'You mean, to avoid anything erotic?' She gave a forced laugh.

'For example, to avoid anything erotic. I do not wish to desire you, if that isn't too impolite.'

The forced smile did not leave her face. Her irony was too obvious to hide her bitterness. 'Yes, you looked as if you had had a few strenuous nights when you came into the hall.'

'Offended after all?'

The forced smile had stiffened when she said, 'Friendship. In short, you need friendship after days of passion.' He said, 'Perhaps it's as simple as that. Why should it be degrading to be unmasked? What does it mean really: unmasked, seen through, given oneself away? As if the whole purpose was pretence, to protect oneself.'

The forced smile gradually gave way to a slightly surprised expression. 'Do you know, I've simply never thought about that,' she said.

He said, and now all awkward tension had gone from his voice as well, 'I've often wished someone would say that sentence, someone I liked, or wanted to like, or I myself — afterwards, after I've been an impatient know-all. It's so seldom anyone admits that a simple idea is new to them; it's as if it would be embarrassing.'

And now, when the one suddenly no longer wanted to go one better than the other, the bar fell quiet. They looked about them, at the comically masculine interior, with isolated fragments of ships on the walls, a capstan, two lanterns, a length of mast and plenty of rope. He looked at her soft cheeks with the strong cheek-bones below a reddish-brown sweep of hair, the slightly childlike, large hands resting on the edge of the table, straightforward and honest, completely lacking that plump sleekness that made so many women's hands repulsive in his eyes. Like her feet, he thought, and realized that he had noticed them as they were walking through the park in the shade of the trees, on their way from the hall which was unfamiliar to them both, to a bar which appeared tempting when one came from such a place; he had noticed that she walked with her feet pointing straight ahead, and that they were not small and doll-like and that she did not trip along, making no progress, but that she walked with purpose, yet still gracefully. He said, 'I suppose you attend meetings like that purely out of duty, because you're a psychologist practising some kind of social work, welfare perhaps; something you have even graver doubts about than the infallible, omniscient interpretation of human actions which you're trained to do under the label of psychology.'

And yet again he felt a pleasurable twinge of satisfaction when she did not confirm his guesswork with a surprised, how on earth ...! On the contrary she smiled, somewhat wearily, 'Is it so obvious?' And he wanted to say, not where you're concerned, not you; all the others, but not you. He said, 'Just that you don't appear completely natural as part of the décor at popular lectures.'

'And do you always classify people in that way? According to how they fit in, I mean?'

'I don't classify them. It's more often the other way round, unfortunately. If you think it sounds arrogant ...'

'Not arrogant. Categorical. As if you make notes and then finish with it.'

He looked at this stranger. These were topics from bygone days, from times that ought to have been forgotten.

'A short while ago,' he said, 'you wanted to be rid of me. You were thinking, The things one gets mixed up in — or something of the sort.'

'Really! And what am I thinking now?'

'You may be a little irritated that all your irony is lost on me. It *is* irritating. I must tell you, I've experienced so much irony, I mean as an attitude to life. Otherwise you're not thinking very much about me particularly. Only that the unpleasant side of this meeting is not so much to the fore any longer.'

And again there came that calm feeling of well-being between them, seeming to take its place, like an observer, a being behind them which said: the advantage of a little experience, a slight lack of illusion, is that one has no need to blow one's own trumpet. Most acquaintance begins with dissimulation.

'I have the feeling I know you,' he said. 'It sounds a bit banal, but I'm not afraid of that. You give me a feeling of security. That hasn't happened to me for very long time. I'm sure that's not a flattering thing to say to a young woman, but I'm not much afraid of that either.'

'What *are* you afraid of?'

'You ask as if you'd really like an answer. No, no, that doesn't often happen between people. I'd like to tell you something. Naturally that sounds self-centred.'

'And you're not afraid of that either?'

'Not in relation to you, that's how it is. One can be so irresolute. I've been alone for a long time and have embarked on something. I went into the hall because there was shade there.'

'Only for that reason?'

'Only for that reason. I met you. It's up to you whether we shall meet again.'

She sat silent for a while, looking at her two hands lying in front of her on the table. They were not playing with her glass; they were tranquil. She said, 'In that case we shall meet.'

3

This is what happened the first time he visited her. It was a kind of lodging house, but did not call itself that. From the first time he asked for Sonja he was always given a warm welcome. He brought flowers with him and introduced himself. 'My name is Matias Roos. I'm calling on one of your lodgers.' The owner, Mrs Skarseth, was lavish with her praise from the start.

'Sonja's such a sweet-natured girl,' she said. 'Above all, sweet-natured. She has plenty of good qualities, certainly, but I appreciate a sweet nature. In our day there is so little of it. But please don't call them lodgers. The young people who live with me treat my house as their home; they are my friends. I sometimes call them 'the gang', have you ever heard anything so silly, and while I remember I'll put the flowers in water, lovely flowers, Sonja isn't at home but she'll be here soon, I'm expecting her, we know each other's habits in this house. Your name is Roos? An unusual name. You're a foreigner perhaps? So many fugitives come here, they look on my house as their home — all of them. I'm very broad-minded. They have names ending in -vitch and -ski, we're all broad-minded here, many of them come. Roos is an interesting name, something foreign about it. Perhaps you're a fugitive? Everyone's welcome here.'

'Yes, I am perhaps a bit of a fugitive,' he admitted, happy about this possibility.

She said, 'I understand. I understand you completely, sit down for a while. I see you're wondering about that picture over there. No, it's not supposed to represent anything, not in that sense. I read so much into it. I think one should be open to contemporary trends. You can't stop progress. My husband was a colonel, as perhaps you know — yes, that's him in the photograph, as a matter of fact it's not a good one, he couldn't stand modern art. What in the world is that supposed to mean? he said. Have you ever heard of such a thing — mean! But I was broad-minded. You can get along with one another without agreeing on everything. In fact, my husband and I never agreed, and as for that picture, it has its own story. It was painted by a gentleman who lived in this house, a guest, a talented man in many ways, he left several pictures here, he earned his living as a bar pianist at the Ambassador, you must know the Ambassador? A first class place. I go out very little myself, my husband was not much in favour of going out either, but the Ambassador is an excellent place, entertaining with all the foreigners who go there. But this gentleman was the bar pianist at the Ambassador — a highly gifted man. And then he had such a good relationship with his brother — who is still my guest from that day to this. A splendid relationship between two brothers of good family. He's gifted too, a kind of architect or something of the sort, they call it designing, he's drawn the sketch for a fork with a very thin handle. My word, these artists, where do they find all their ideas? And when I say good family I mean substantial folk, their father was a tinsmith here in town. And then imagine two such gifted artists, sons of an ordinary tinsmith by the name of Forfang, heaven knows, he might really be a Treschow or a Bernadotte by birth. And where Sonja's concerned, she might be my own child. Imagine, so self-assured, so idealistic, she leaves her good home, excellent parents, he's a civil servant, leaves it in protest because her liberal views could not accept all the formality and narrow-mindedness in such a home. Well, in fact her mother is fairly broad-minded, believe you me.' And now Mrs Skarseth leaned towards him mysteriously and whispered, 'She comes here — her mother — when she knows Sonja's at the welfare office. She brings a bag of eggs or somesuch, two grilled chops and asks me to let her have them as if from the house, in deception you understand, for Sonja would certainly be offended, she would be outraged at such secret concern for her; and God forgive me, but I can say it to you, her mother is really touching, she brings a couple of pairs of stockings and puts them in Sonja's drawer, or some clothes on a shelf, placing them there casually, as if they were things our Sonja has scattered about, she doesn't keep track of her things, they don't, these modern intellectual women. I'll tell you something: she can't bear to be provided for, Sonja, she can't bear the thought of anyone taking care of her, showing concern for her — she's one of these completely free women, if you understand what I mean, and I'm not saying it in any malicious sense, but she's a person who loves liberty; but with all those committees she belongs to, she sees scarcely anyone besides fugitives, so that's why I permitted myself the remark about the name, about your name, not meaning to be personal, I'm sure you understand that. I look on our Sonja as a daughter. That isn't her name, her name's Katrine, she called herself Sonja in protest — after a play or something, I think. She left them, she left her home, there's supposed to have been a violent scene — did I tell you her father was a civil servant? *Is.* He's still alive. Both parents. A blow for them. But her mother is understanding, broad-minded in her fashion, a mother hen. I know what it means to be a mother, I had a daughter myself...'

Mrs Skarseth looked about her. She had a habit of looking about her, as if she had to ascertain those simple objects that belong to reality: a basket chair, an old-fashioned easy chair, a table with a copper surface, all of it thrown together in the hope that it would look like what is called an entrance hall. He remained standing while she spoke, but sat down in the basket chair when she gestured, which also permitted her to sit.

'I'm telling you the truth, I'm relieved and happy that Sonja has found a friend, she's too wrapped up in her work. I think I mentioned that her father is a civil servant, she has something of the same — a devotion to duty, well, I don't know ... I'm a supporter of devotion to duty. But too much is too much, don't you think? She gets so wrapped up in everything, it worries me, I often think at night when I can't sleep: Sonja, I think, if you were my daughter I'd see to it that you didn't wear yourself out with all this ... irrelevant business. Did I say irrelevant? You mustn't misunderstand me. It's important, it's an unavoidable duty that someone should provide for — well, for everything our society cannot manage to do, for reasons that I'll not talk about, important that someone should look after things — yes, things. Of course, she's a trained psychologist too,

Sonja, I can't imagine a more splendid career than that of psychology, understanding people. But as I say, too much is too much. There's something distant about Sonja, something — excuse me for saying so — something dreamy. Isn't she a young woman, almost a girl? Hasn't she the right to — I'm sure you understand what I mean, I saw at once that you're an understanding person. And doesn't Sonja have the right to ... So that's why I was glad when you turned up at the door and asked for our Sonja, for my lodger, as you put it. You couldn't know any better, but ask Sonja, I tell you, ask Sonja. Lodger ...!'

There was a nervous naiveté about Mrs Skarseth which put him at ease at once. He stretched out his legs in the tiny space and offered her a cigarette and a light for them both. She said, as if dreaming:

'I observe these things, a young girl, her conscientious mother, forced to stifle her anxiety, and a father whose heart may be torn with anxiety for his daughter, for everything, for his prestige. I imagine these people, each of them without any desire to hurt one another. But what happens? They do hurt one another. Once I asked my husband, the late Colonel Skarseth, to take a glass out to the pantry, I did it without thinking, it was his glass, he drank quite a lot — no, I had nothing against it, I was understanding, but can you guess what his answer was? Women's work, he replied. He said more than that. He said that if the rot had begun to sneak into the family circle, God knew what things would come to. Those were his words. I took out the glass. I took his glasses in and out. When I look back at my marriage, I see that it mainly consisted of carrying glasses in and out. And bottles, bottles as well. But don't think I'm complaining. He was an affectionate man in his way, he was a colonel, remember. Just not very *good-natured*. And now Sonja's father, the civil servant, well, I don't know him, but I've seen him, somebody pointed him out to me on the street. So much the opposite of my husband — in every way the opposite. This one's a dry man, small, quick, matter-of-fact in everything, you can see it in his pace — measured. A watchful man. And yet they resemble each other. In their watchfulness, if you see what I mean. In not daring to let anyone come close to them, not anyone. The colonel, my husband, was big. In his youth he had been unusually strong, a farmer's son, he could carry a sack of oats or whatever on his back from the cowshed or wherever they keep that kind of thing — rye or oats, he could carry the sack on his back to ... well, as far as he had to. And yet a weak man in his way. Just like Sonja's father, just like that civil servant, a strong man in his way, even though he may seem small and wizened when he walks past you. What was I trying to say? I think there is often more *potency* — note my words — in a dried up little man like that, than in the whole of, I almost said a regiment. And, as I said, that's precisely why I'm so happy for Sonja's sake as I look at you now, a visiting, attentive admirer, because, as I believe I said, she's so wrapped up in her work, in — well, in all this, call it her hobby. Her freethinking — she has no use for her freethinking. I think of my own young days; if a young girl had had all that liberty, all this desire for liberty — we'd have used it. I tell you straight out: we'd have used it. What do they do nowadays, young people? They shut themselves in with their passionate sense of duty as if — well, as if that's all there is. And what does that lead to? What do they get out of their freethinking? I wouldn't say it's wasted, I don't want to exaggerate. But I still think it's sad.'

He said, 'What's so sad about Sonja?'

She sat silent for a long time, unused to being asked. Then she said, 'That she has no friend, only friends.'

He said, 'Mrs Skarseth, you're a wise woman. Do they listen to you here in your house?'

Again she sat silent. 'They listen and they don't listen,' she said. 'Perhaps I talk too much, I don't know, it's more than twenty years since my husband died, and he didn't listen to me very often. I'm surrounded by people. I'm happy.'

'Did you wish for your husband's death?' he asked.

She did not gasp. He observed her very carefully. She did not even pretend to be surprised or offended.

'I've often asked myself that,' she said finally.

'And the answer?'

'Probably no. I realize it may seem dishonest, it may *be* dishonest, I mean untrue. Why do you ask?'

'Do you think that the wish, if you had it, might have mattered — I mean, since you have treated me with a certain openness, do you think that if you had had to answer your question in the affirmative — honest as you are — that the wish itself ...?'

'I don't know.'

'Or the fear that — a fear that was continually fed, almost like a passion ...?'

'What do you mean?'

'That supposing he had been ill, let us say for a long time, and you surrounded yourself with words — or with thoughts for that matter — such as "It would be best for him" — that this could influence the course of the illness?'

'I feel as if I've met you before. That cigarette case ...?'

'I inherited it.'

'Beautiful. I inherited too. A little. A few trifles. No, I didn't wish for his death. I missed him.'

'But not any more?'

'I missed him while he was alive.'

'And since then?'

'Yes, now and again. I miss him. His apparent brutality — I saw through that. He was a child. Apprehensive.'

'And you, weren't you apprehensive?'

'Women of my generation were filled with duty. Day and night, I tell you. Day — and night. If only one's duties had been fulfilled. I admit it; I, too, was very conscientious.'

'And he wasn't?'

'It wasn't a question of duty for him. It was a question of rights. You can renounce your rights. Not your duties.'

She lit a cigarette from the open case. Then she said, 'Colonel Skarseth was a man who was very neglectful of his rights.'

'Did you say, after his death, that it was a good thing matters had turned out as they did?'

'I know you mean it kindly, you're a candid person. I'm glad for Sonja's sake. I'll tell you honestly, she needs a friend. Yes, maybe I said something of the sort — that it was best for him. I still think so. I've seen many fugitives with that same — what shall I call it? — that incurable arrogance, a stubbornness in the face of fate, which they recognize themselves, and dislike. You thought I was a helper by nature — a friend of all who suffer? No, no, I see you no longer

31

believe it. I am perhaps a friend of those who cause their own suffering.'

'What do you do about it?'

'What does one do about anything? One lives, one exists. My broad-mindedness — you thought I was talking a lot about that, you were thinking, What an old nincompoop, isn't Sonja coming soon, so I can get rid of her?'

'For once you're wrong.'

'I take note with pleasure that I am mistaken, if you say so. This sense of what has been left undone — that's what haunts us. We go so far as to do what we don't want to do — what nobody wants us to do — in order to get things done. We look around us, at all the successful people, at all those we believe to be a success, and say to ourselves: They get things done, get something done yourself, get it done, whatever it may be. Oh, yes, I know about that. I do it myself. There's a lot of foolishness in the world.'

'I don't miss Sonja now. I'd be grateful if you went on talking to me.'

'About what? Oh well — you're right. Sometimes I do miss having someone to listen to me. The problem is, one has one's ideas, one's ideas and experience. But what then? My husband used to say, to curb me, "Mind your own business." He always said that in English, I don't know why, perhaps there's something English about the idea? But what does it mean? You asked me some questions a little while ago, extraordinary questions one might call them, but I don't know, they didn't surprise me. But something about them was new to me: all this about wishing. Do we humans do anything else? Can we avoid wishing? It may be the humblest thing we can permit ourselves. *Action* was what my husband the colonel always said. Nothing but action was worthwhile. But what then? When you're forced at the same time to leave everything to others, to those trained for it. I wish for a great deal, let me tell you, I suppose I continually wish the best for everybody. Perhaps it is none of my business. Once upon a time everything was ordered according to rank, such and such a wife had to sit thus and so at a public event. My husband set great store by that, he was a military man and that's what used to happen, it was another time. Nowadays only politicians and the armed forces seem to think like that. It's a bit alarming, too, since they're the people who govern the world. But even wishing was not the business of someone who had nothing to do with it — me. Once I was the manager of a very stylish establishment for social events, Beaulieu it was called, down on the coast; wedding receptions and all kinds of parties were held there, but mostly weddings. It was a profitable business, and can you imagine, I was so touched, I was touched every time a bridal couple came in through the door and everyone sat down at the banqueting table. Why did I give up the business? The songs. They made me so nervous, I can almost say I was driven crazy. The same songs, or almost the same, to the same tunes — all of them so full of hope and confidence in the future. I think I must have listened to two thousand wedding songs in my time. But all that confidence got on my nerves. Song and cliché found their way into the furthest corners of Beaulieu — it was as if they haunted the rooms long after each reception was over, as if even the chairs were singing in the early morning light when we went round, dead tired, tidying up. And when one occasionally heard rumours about how all these marriages were going, then all that confident trust, all their future ... well, believe it or not, but I was seized with such sorrow, such sorrow, let me tell you — for the bridal couple, for humanity. I couldn't stand it any more. It seemed as if any kind of expression of happiness carried disappointment with it as a possibility, almost a certainty, a painful warning — that was all happiness was. It became so bad that I would see a healthy young man beside his bride, and think: one fine day he'll have prostate trouble, and what good is a man when they put a catheter in him — put a hard, painful rubber tube into that dead scrap of flesh which was once his proud organ, the delight of his wife? And it was the same with everything. And I thought: Is it the duty of the wife, after all those years, to service her poor husband in that situation too? There's one good thing about you, the Colonel would say when he was in the mood, you were born into the proletariat, you can get used to anything. And perhaps he was right. Although we weren't really working class; we were gentle-folk, but extremely poor, that's true. I might put it that the Colonel lifted me up a peg, as they say. Do you think I dared tell him about some of the most delightful moments of my childhood?

They were when I was sent to the Salvation Army soup kitchen on Thursdays with a soup pail. It was cold and dark and dangerous in the narrow alleyways with only one weak gaslight. And it was slippery, so slippery. It was important not to spill soup from the brimming pail. But that was almost impossible, the paths were so steep and dark. I had a blue coat at that time, a woollen coat with a collar of rabbit fur and a thick hem. And of course I slipped with the pail, and spilt soup on the coat at the bottom of the hem. And I remember it as if it had been yesterday, how I put the pail down on the staircase and tore open the frozen edge of my coat with my teeth and gradually sucked up the pea soup as it thawed against my mouth. Yes, those were pleasant moments, but he didn't want to hear about them, not about anything of that kind, not about the bad men who came up to me in the dark to show off their anatomy to little girls. Not that it really harmed us; well, I don't know, some of them did nothing but read about film stars for the rest of their lives. I understand them, I read about people who live on the sunny side myself. Perhaps there's a wish in that too. If there is — who does it harm? Ourselves. We lose our power to act. But wasn't taking action precisely what we were *not* supposed to do, we women of my generation? It was none of our business. It was our business to ponder, to dream. I'm not saying this in order to complain. I'll regret saying it, too. But what of it? In any case I regret — everything. Besides, it's boring you.'

'It doesn't bore me,' he said, and offered her another cigarette. 'You said you had a daughter?'

'I had. I have, for that matter.'

She got to her feet and stood for a while, and again it was as if she was noting the objects in the room, the dark maw of the hearth, the two rifles crossed above it. It occurred to him that perhaps this woman never really believed in her own surroundings, her own circumstances, that she was in a state of eternal flight — she too.

'It's not what you're thinking,' she said quietly, 'as perhaps you *are* thinking, that my daughter got into trouble, as they say, that she means the defeat of all my hopes and wishes. My daughter is a teacher up north, a useful person, happy maybe. We write to each other now and again. She could marry. In the past she was very good-looking. What did she do? She liberated herself. She has a child and makes no secret of it. But have you noticed that the unmarried mother almost always has only one child? A kind of admission of a false move seems to lie in that simple fact. I think her child was a manifesto, that her unmarried state is a manifesto, perhaps even her teaching career a protest. Against what? Against the Colonel? No, against me! Perhaps that's rather bitter, but I believe it to be so. And in that case it seems to me that to carry out such a manifesto is no liberation after all, but rather a confirmation of the conventions they're fighting. One cannot live solely in protest, a woman can't do that. Do you know Acharya Vinoba Bhave? He's just called Vinoba. It's so easy to ridicule these women who get enthusiastic about everything Indian, and I'm sure they are often ridiculous. But a few years ago, a couple of years after Vinoba had set out on his enormous journey which included the whole vastness of India, with the purpose of persuading the rich landowners to transfer some of their property to the peasants, two years after this marvellous start to a mighty venture, the Rajah of Ranka in Bihar announced that he was giving 11,000 acres to one of his workers and 2,500 acres to another. Vinoba asked him, "How much will you give me, then?" "As much as you want," answered the Rajah. "I have 100,000 acres of uncultivated land and 7,000 acres that I have cultivated myself." "Normally," said Vinoba, "I demand only one-sixth, but in this case I will ask you for the 100,000 acres of uncultivated land." The Rajah replied, "As you wish." And it was done. What's the point in telling you this? I'm not sure. But it's like a breath from a completely different world, a different mentality, a way of communicating between people which leaps over centuries of detailed planning and allows pure perception of matters to be valid instead. Absolute perception of matters, if you understand what I mean — independent of logic, of all reason. Perhaps we women are inclined to a certain enthusiasm for this absolute perception. What is logical, reasonable — doesn't seem to have led to any result, seen with our eyes, with mine ... My husband would have called this kind of argument flight, flights of fancy. And perhaps he would have been right. Some people may be as it were fugitives, marching on the same spot, simply because it's their nature for all I know. Maybe from habit. Well, well, I got on to this because you mentioned the word *wish*. Some people live in the wish. It's more than hope — in a way more active. But it's less than fulfilment. *That* doesn't seem to be part of it ... Perhaps you think I leap from one thing to another? A young man who lives here, Esterhazy, a Hungarian, says Mrs Skarseth leaps "from one thing to one thing", "nobody can hold on to her" says Esterhazy. A talented young man. But hasn't he himself leaped from both one thing and another. Once he was a communist and almost lost his life because of it; now he designs window displays and gives lectures to charitable ladies about his mistreated country.'

'He says you leap from one thing to one thing?'

'Of course he means from one thing to another. His language isn't very fluent yet, but admirable all the same.'

'You mentioned planning — that people make plans and carry them out more or less out of a commitment to the action itself?'

She looked at him for a long time. 'Did I say that? Perhaps I did. I have a certain fear of plans, perhaps a fear of action. It calls for such enormous consequences. Forgive me, but I think nearly everything human beings set in motion comes to grief; what was meant well often harms the very people one wants to help. One takes action at the wrong place. Or doesn't take action at all. That can be premeditated too — an action. People hurt others and themselves. One can't envisage what they wanted to achieve.'

'You mentioned your daughter?'

'Precisely. And my husband. I've never behaved justly towards anyone. Perhaps I've never achieved anything. You mentioned *the wish*, the power of the wish. It's true, I've wished a great deal. Perhaps I wished for the wrong things. Oh, my goodness, I'm tiring you with my talk. It was because you turned up, it was the thought of Sonja. I don't even dare to wish anything for her now. I only wish she'd come home.'

A key was put in the door. Sonja stood there in her yellow suit. She took in the scene with one glance — the flowers, everything.

'Any introductions are superfluous,' she said. 'Do you know, Antoinette, what this man believes? That people ought to be *punished*. He believes in punishment, isn't that fantastic? He believes in punishment for its own sake. I think he longs for it.'

Antoinette Skarseth had stood up as soon as Sonja came in. Her glance at the young woman was like a caress. Then her glance met that of this man whom she did not know. There lay deep mutual trust in it, a confidence which expressed itself without qualification. She laughed good-naturedly and left them alone.

That was what happened the first time he visited Sonja.

4

All this is to his advantage, so he's drifting away from me now: he has no need of me. How is it that only in our painful moments do we feel whole? He was intimately close to me when Mrs Skarseth talked about her daughter. That guilt-seeking, truthful person was lying at that point, for fear of something, and he knew it. He felt her fear and was embarrassed. He looked for help in the rest of himself then, in order to avoid being dragged into the deception, into that trance that the confider imposes on the confidant. She mentioned something about an inheritance as well, a few small things, after the Colonel I suppose? But didn't her daughter inherit? So this colonel can't have owned very much. But all the money she had earned at Beaulieu — he couldn't help such thoughts occurring to him and demanding room for a moment. The daughter — that was the only thing Mrs Skarseth had tried to hide. And a teacher's miserable salary in a small town in the far north was all it was!

But that soon passed. He drifted away from us again, his ego expanded and became cocksure in the pleasure of the exchange of confidences. He entered into that secure state of well-being that results from switching off one's personality in favour of a stranger's small ills. It creates affinity. But was he really interested?

Difficult to decide. We have two ears and listen with both; there is a central place inside us where impressions meet and are given shape. Persons who are talked about acquire faces. The Colonel's face — unlike the photograph on the mantelpiece, a face *beneath* the stern face of achievement in the oval frame; a wounded face, not that of the wounded warrior, but of an exhausted afternoon drinker who finds boredom at the bottom of each glass, and without hesitation tries another in the hope that ... that maybe she'll die one day, the Madam?

Her garrulity must have seemed to him like interminable chatter. Her preoccupation with the world outside, that restless conscience concerning the distorted course of events — oh, how it must have seemed naive to the point of idiocy to a Colonel Skarseth, used to taking for granted himself and everything that was his. Can Colonel Skarseth doubt his own existence? If so, he would have to take one of the rifles down from the wall and make the procedure as brief as possible. But does it occur to him? Of course not. All his life he has been in the right. He is in the right in advance, even about matters and ideas which have never crossed his mind before; automatically in the right in everything which opposes Mrs Skarseth's notions, her theories and fears. The trouble with Antoinette, he would say, musing over the rim of his enormous glass, is that ... But he will not so much as approach a definition. For of course everything about Antoinette is wrong. In his eyes she is like a ship which has never set sail, but nevertheless goes on gurgling about the dangers and difficulties of the sea. 'Doesn't know what she's talking about!' the Colonel has said to himself every day for twenty years. *He* knows all about the things on which he keeps silent: an enormous void, brimful with omniscience.

And in this respect Matias Roos feels at ease with Antoinette Skarseth in her restless speculation; he does not need the aid of the self, he is secure in his passive complicity. It's just this business of the daughter; then he was close to me, he was suffering. The fact is, when a widow talks about her adult daughter, self-supporting, consistent in her behaviour and happy in her work, she recognizes her daughter's lie, senses her suffering, and falls back on lies herself.

'We write to each other now and again.'

How many letters has she received over the years? Oh, the pile is not too thick for the narrowest drawer in her writing desk. And those that are there are frequently read, carefully replaced every time in each yellow envelope which is worn at the edges from the many times she has done so.

And now Sonja? No, there we are uncertain. The development of their relationship has not followed any kind of pattern. It's not the same as with the women in whose company he drowns himself for a few days and nights; then he keeps me completely outside.

But with Sonja he wants to keep me outside, too; he allows no thoughts to disturb him, because he is clinging to what he calls destiny. He does it to forget his insecurity about many things, but especially about what he very much wanted to forget during that first period after he fled from this house: the child on the road, that piece of knitting flapping and flapping in the wind. He did report himself to the police, but they sent him away after some meaningless cross-examination. They insisted that there had been no child, no little girl who had been killed. What they could not deny — but they did not know that — was his guilt. Sonja is able to keep it away from him. A strange girl. She almost takes care of him. He has probably made a mental note of Mrs Skarseth's advice, that she cannot bear anyone to show concern for her.

But can't she? that's one of the reasons why he flees from me in this respect; because he doesn't want to find out that perhaps Mrs Skarseth knows nothing.

They went out together frequently that summer, and shared the pleasures of the city. The theatre presented extremely light entertainment which could not give rise to any discussion. The restaurants offered plenty of empty tables and excessive solicitude on the part of the waiters, until the foreigners arrived and commandeered their attention for the sake of their tips.

Later on they would stroll along the streets, visiting suburbs that were so old that they had forgotten them, or so new that they were still undiscovered, and small cafés that took on a magical glow simply by being featureless. They discovered that two people who are new to each other can discover something in everything, that the one can see with the other's eyes. He thought: I would have called this being in love if it had not been out of the question, so decidedly out of the question. They travelled on trains above and below ground, and everything pleased them.

But they did not walk in the surrounding countryside. As if by mutual agreement they avoided it. Once he remarked, casually, 'Everyone's there at this time of year.' That decided it. They could continue conversations which had not yet begun, both of them having understood their point of departure. Thus:

She: 'I thought that men, at any rate, would get terribly tired of her.'

He: 'On the contrary. Mrs Skarseth is the only person I've met who doesn't react to anything with scepticism, not to persons, not to events.'

'Do you even think she seems logical?'

'Yes. And full of good sense. Esterhazy is a genius at expressing himself incorrectly in the right way. He has said she leaps from one thing to one thing.'

She laughed, gravely. 'And what is this one thing?'

'Her daughter.'

'The teacher? Johanna?'

'Yes. Is her name Johanna?'

'She's come home only on one occasion. A tall girl, above average, quite good-looking. She's inherited features from the Colonel without resembling him. I admire her.'

'Is it in fact such an achievement to have a child?'

'I didn't say so. But she is at least consistent.'

'And that's admirable?'

She laughed. 'You do have a way of belittling things. Do you know, I think you prefer people to be completely passive.'

'On the contrary. No — I'm not sure. I've just broken away from a passivity that looked as if it was going to become lifelong.'

'Broken away to what?'

'I didn't say to, I said from. I'm waiting for a demonstration that actions are only to the good. Something happened immediately — a child. I know I've been intending to tell you about it. I need to.'

'I've been waiting.'

They were sitting in the empty stands in the Amusement Park. It was evening. He said, 'A thing changes its character by being told. You're the only person — and yet ... I've told you that I left a good friend. That's not quite true. I left myself. Before that I had fled for a while, but that was a very long time ago. I was afraid of every departure, of all action. Most of it is painful.'

'You and Mrs Skarseth —! She never talks to me about Johanna.'

Or it might happen like this when he went to fetch her at the end of the brief office hours she kept for the good of some social cause or other, and they ate their light summer meal in a cafeteria with plastic-topped tables and stainless steel cutlery.

She: 'At least you know something about me: that I spend time in an office and then come away again.'

He: 'And about me you know — nothing. There's nothing to know. Today, for instance, I've been walking about the streets since early morning. And I went to the law courts and listened to a court case.'

'And what did you experience?'

'Very little. Do you know, one summer, during my childhood, the best summer in my life, I must have been six years old, things happened all the time. I know that, because many things since then seem to be an echo of something forgotten. But it must date from that summer.'

'And you don't remember anything about it?'

'Only one thing, that a wagtail was sitting on a log that had jammed in the middle of a waterfall. The water sprayed up in a fan of water drops against the log and formed a small rainbow. The wagtail was sitting in the middle of the rainbow.'

'The court case today — what was it about?'

'A woman, a small matter, but maybe decisive for her. She was accused of shop-lifting, of all things. Caught red-handed, as they say, as well as having been observed many times. When her house was searched they found all kinds of things there — eighteen umbrellas!'

'A kleptomaniac, in other words?'

'A lot of people are sceptical about that idea. But she denied that she was the person who had been arrested, who had been observed, who had all these things in her house. Denied it repeatedly, with an obstinacy so desperate that it was beyond all reason.'

'And what did they do with her?'

'I don't know. I left. The point is that she was in good faith. I think one holds to such faith as one has need of.'

'But then there would be no difference between truth and falsehood!'

'There isn't so much difference as is usually believed. She had absolutely no need of punishment. — But can't you see that? There are thousands of possibilities for dividing people into two kinds. One of them is innate innocence. A broker in Boston, an important man, one of the most powerful men and brokers in the world, gets up at seven o'clock, eats his frugal breakfast — grilled kippers and coffee — drives to the office in an ancient Oldsmobile, drinks one small glass of whisky every night and helps hordes of small investors through his precision, his vision if you like, in this one area, supported by the rumour of his simple way of life. This man is by nature without guilt. If anyone said to him, "You're one of those qualified self-deluded fellows who will certainly go to hell," he wouldn't answer that he didn't believe in eternal torment — no, for he certainly does believe in it. But he would be virtuous enough as he was, with proof to back him up, that general testimony which has acquitted him in advance. In addition he gives to charity.'

'Which indicates that your broker in Boston is a splendid man.'

'Precisely. What then? Another poor soul comes before a court of law, real or imaginary. His need to be sentenced is in him already. He is guilty, whatever the argument. Why not sentence him? Everyone knows it would be the best solution for him. But it would not be the best solution for the jury. They wouldn't sleep at night. This man, whose personality is guilty, is acquitted to face a life sentence, instead of a sentence limited to, let us say, the twelve years he needs.'

'Your theories would produce a strange legal system.'

'Don't mention legal systems, don't mention theories — not you. You play your social games and fight petty sinners energetically from a comic sense of injustice. I don't suppose it harms anyone. Who cares?'

'So I'd do better to sit with my hands in my lap?'

'An excellent thing to do with hands. Do you know why she was called Antoinette? One of her ancestors was a French migrant quarryman in sandstone. The family came here from Fredericia. The father abandoned them; he left home because the weather was so fine.'

'She tells you things like that?'

'Johanna doesn't know that either. But I think she ought to know about it. Perhaps it would explain to her the urge she feels up there beneath the midnight sun, to abandon everything ... No, no, you're right. I don't know her. I was told her name only a short while ago, by you. But a mother can sense her daughter's unhappiness from a great distance, even though she doesn't understand her anxieties at home. So she fantasizes her situation into consistency.'

'It's remarkable how interested you are in this Johanna.'

'Yes. She's the bearer of misfortune for herself, for others. There's a great deal of muddle inside Mrs Skarseth's head. You asked me once whether I thought her stupid. Quite the opposite. But the muddle originates in a daughter who was once a kind of symbol for her — of some kind of liberation, something to do with women, something that would perhaps have suited *her*, if things had worked out that way. And she has guided this daughter — or not guided her, it doesn't really matter — but she has *desired* her to go in a certain direction, let us say in the direction of perseverance, the direction of independence and consistency if you like, of determined struggle. One day it will take its revenge.'

'*She* will take her revenge, do you mean — Johanna?'

'Yes. On someone, perhaps herself. That daughter has a fund of latent envy, which increases from day to day.'

'Envy — of whom?'

'You, perhaps. I believe she hates you.'

At the edge of town stood an old mansion. The buildings were white, and in a dominating position. In the course of time wings had been added, outgrowths with glossy paint. But despite all the destruction, the main house now stood like a monument in the landscape. An avenue of hundreds of lime trees led up to it, turning the place into an aristocratic island, fenced in on three sides by blocks of flats, old wooden houses, and nursery gardens ... They often strolled up there. Then he would call her the Baroness and she would pretend to carry a parasol. When they reached the enormous courtyard, where an oak tree presided in the centre like a mighty

God Shiva with numerous arms stretching out over the world, they glanced up cautiously at the empty windows, in case someone was watching them. She said that if his Lordship the Baron would permit it, she would take the air once more, and he replied that if it entertained her he would offer to escort her, unless she wished to distract her thoughts. Perhaps he should call for the coachman instead and order him to bring out the cariole. 'Hither, Jens!' he called with abandon. 'What makes him bide so long in the straw?'

Then they had to hurry, for fear anyone had heard them.

One evening she was in no hurry. There was such a fine drizzle that it failed to dampen their clothes, but a shimmer of silver lay over trees and people, over the old pony-carriage which was drawn up in front of the coach house for all eternity. She paused and said, almost coldly, 'This seems to me to be like love.' They stood facing each other for a long time, close together, their clothes in symbolic contact. Something spoke within him — *I* spoke within him ... though it was not speech, but he raised both hands and grasped her upper arms, close to her shoulders, cautiously, very cautiously. It's only that, in what ought to be self-forgetfulness, *I* intervene. It seemed like hesitation, she noticed it, slipped out of his grasp, he followed, but she slipped away. This turned into a curious walk under the lime trees with their silver shimmer: one of them walking backwards with small crayfish movements, one walking forwards, with the false energy of apparent determination. Was she already on her way to becoming one of us, a part of us, too close to be loved? *She* did not know, for each of her impulses was a reflex, she did not know from what, she knew nothing except that she was someone who takes the initiative and who ceases to take it at precisely the same moment. Thus they wound their way down through the dim light of the avenue, like the striking pistons of an engine, the one stroke releasing the other. Then they paused after all, and stood, their cheeks touching, for a long time. There was an inexpressible resignation in this passive approach. They wished to increase it, and did not; they wished to diminish it, to bring it to an end; they shared a perfect, common will, but it lacked energy. Neither was the hunter, neither the hunted. He knew that if he ... but he didn't really consider it, for they were one body one soul, simply through this touch which at that moment was supremely intimate and yet without any compelling incentive towards action.

Afterwards they walked for a long time. The drizzle ceased, it became dark, the moon came out. It paled, it grew light in the north-east, a sky like blue milk, and later golden towards daylight. For a while they had been walking hand in hand. Not even that any more. But the touch lived in their bodies, in their shared body; and the proximity of their minds was more than a closeness: it was an exchange. She was him, or the wholeness in a 'him' she was seeking. As for him — now he was also me, he was his whole self, seeking nothing, his desire complete, but without demands. It was directed towards a companionship in which she was no more an object than the whole they formed together.

Once they halted in full sunshine. Milk vans rattled downhill on their way to the town centre, lorries loaded with vegetables thundered past. He said, 'Do you think one can learn anything about love — from experience, for instance?'

She said, 'No, I think I know everything.'

'About us?'

'Not about you, not about myself either. About our love.'

And after a while, when they were sitting in the unavoidable cafeteria, he said, 'What do you know about our love?'

'That it's greater than something but smaller than something else.'

'What stands between us?'

'You won't tell me that. Or you can't. If you wanted me to be that part of you which — which you lack, I would want that, even that, although love should be between two, surely? Or can it be everything? I don't know. I think it has a myriad forms, but no pattern. Perhaps most people believe there must be a pattern and that's the reason that ... no, no, I don't know. I think love must be extraordinary, must have the right to create its own pattern. I don't know. I love you.'

'*I* love *you*.'

Even the enormous content of the words was given no greater weight than the shy movement of their hands above the plastic table top. Words and touch — they were the expression of a search in unknown territory. Neither had been there before. Neither could say: I know, I'm familiar with the way, none of it is so very strange. Neither had the right to the absolute naturalness that lay in the essence of their desire. They could not say with sentimentality: let the inevitable happen!

5

He said, 'At this moment I am in a house in a forest. As I walk out of the house I feel the timber of the wall. It's warm.

The house isn't out of the ordinary, just rather old. And the forest? The lake there isn't out of the ordinary either. Water, a boat, a fishing net. Once a bird got caught in that net, a robin.

Someone is waiting for me there, in that house, in the forest. Not a woman, not a man. Someone. Do I long to be back there? I stayed there in order to long to get away. That seemed to be the function of the house and of myself. There are some birch trees too; they're paler than birches are usually. The firs are heavy and dense. From the pine knoll above you can see the house if you turn round there on your way from it. I did not turn round; if I had, I would have been lost. My departure would have been abandoned, my plan ...

Something crossed my plan, my path. A child crossed the road. I killed it with my insane motor cycle, that wanted to go out into the world. Never mind that it was the fault of the child, or of Daimler the inventor of the motor, or of the state which made the road. A piece of knitting was hanging on the back of a chair. They said I was not guilty. They said there had been no child. They wiped out all traces. I was free, said the authorities.

But am I not in that house in the forest? Don't I live there all the year round, with my insignificant affairs? That's all. Should I tempt fate by changing anything — by causing a change myself? My whole life prior to this is forgotten. All I know about it is that it consisted of change, change for the worse. You have your fugitives, you have me. If only I could give you myself, if only I were truly free. I've never done anything that turned out well. I had every chance, a difficult situation to be in: a freedom of choice that is like coercion. I was an inventor, someone who made discoveries — a curious function. I was in the grip of objects, in the grip of continuity, that is to say, in the grip of human beings: a person who is blamed for the instigations of others, blamed for change. That was why I was hunted that time, singled out and hunted — *that time* which was annulled long ago, which is not allowed to exist. The torment of choice: *that* always takes effect afterwards. Perhaps I was convinced that mankind was supposed to plan, to act, above all, to wish. It must be written down somewhere that we are supposed to wish, since everyone wishes. The desire to wish spreads in us like a disease, however bad our experience is. The certainty of misfortune is enough to create misfortune. The suspicion is enough: the guilt is there in full bloom, when mere hesitation could have kept it in eternal bud — if we had the ability to hesitate, the ability for the perpetually immutable. If only we had the firmness to retain the memory of how strongly we desired calm weather when the storm was raging! You've heard hundreds of accounts about fugitive men, about women with children in their arms or on their backs, who died in ditches, disappeared in dungeons. My account is not dramatic; besides it's been forgotten. There was only one characteristic of all that happened: it lasted so long, oh so long. Some people may have flight in them, perhaps it continues, and it would have begun without any external cause. I don't know, but I believe so. But when in addition ...

May I tell you about the house in the forest? It's red. No, perhaps mostly grey, for much of the red has flaked off, but it's going to be painted, it's always been going to be painted. It lies in a hollow between two low hills, but on a rise between two lakes, a big one where there are fish, and a small dark one with water lilies. It's a large house inside. You must have noticed that some houses are large on the outside, but small when you go in. The House is the opposite. I don't own anything in it, but it's mine. It all belongs to the Farm, but it lies far from the beaten track, six miles or more. I buy everything I need there. Did I say far? Six miles isn't far. Not twelve or sixty either when you know you're coming back. But when you don't know — ?

Often I didn't know. I didn't know when I left. On the contrary, I was certain I was never coming back, certain that something new was about to begin, that I must wish it. I didn't turn round. Nor did I when I left the Farm on my motor cycle. There's an old man there. He keeps an eye on everything, that's all he does. He wanted to ask me ...

But the house. It can wake up in the night and start the day before sunrise; I suppose the whim takes it. I follow the whim; after all, we are one, and the house for its part is amenable. It possesses me, everything in it possesses me. Because everything in the forest and the house was my last resort at one time — the last time. It took away from me the right to wish for anything more, anything beyond itself. Even the fishing net, the boat, the birds in the forest, the ripples on the water at sunrise — once they were my last resort. They stood the test, they held fast. What did I do?

A day came that was different from other days, the way days do. The dawn chorus in the treetops — I didn't hear it, or did I? The jetty and the boat and the lake and the fishing net ... Yes, of course, I saw them. I stood there and saw them; I was there, after all, I stayed behind while I went away. I was not faithless towards them; I didn't mean to be. My will denied them: it wanted to go out and be a will in the world, a plan perhaps. Did I recognize it? Only the commitment to a plan. But misfortune was lodged in my will. I didn't know that then. It was a plan that I took up again, an old one, everything that had been forgotten. It was my unfortunate self who left and resumed a flight I had forgotten. I thought it had ceased; after all, I had forgotten it. But it had only been resting. It wanted to go out and suffer in the world; it desired itself to suffer. I had no mastery over it. For I have heard much about the courage of man and the will of man; I've read about it in books, which have commended this will. One cannot, say the books, let things slide.

But nobody knows how far things have slid until he himself begins to slide. I knew, of course. Children ran across the road, small snotty-nosed kids, wanting to go here, there and everywhere. They, too, must have had a will towards change. And I was steering my motor cycle and had everything under control. A little child like that, I thought, it wants what it wants. Don't give me commonsense reasons about that.

That's what I was thinking. At the same time I watched the morning rise into full day; I saw countless things at the edge of my field of vision. And I saw a house with a lawn with a bench with a woman. She was knitting a garment, it had no sleeves — I saw all that. And I saw the child who wanted to cross the road; she paused, she did and she didn't want to go, just like me. I didn't wish so very much more than not wishing either. I was on the point of stopping and turning back, of taking advantage of this excuse to change my will back into passive hesitation.

But my will wanted something else. I suppose it was longing for affirmation. I hesitated. Then I rode on. The child hesitated, then ran. I knew in advance: this will be your punishment; you are under the law of the self-provoked accident — the accident provoked by minute factors from a long way back, centuries maybe. Here chance wills meet, risen from obscurity; or they might do so. I saw the elderly woman get to her feet, her mouth open; I could see the scream. Afterwards I saw the knitting hanging in the wind over the chair, an armless body flapping, a child's garment, mutilated. A policemen said, "Your imagination is running away with you." But what does a policeman know about my imagination? I have no imagination to speak of; besides, what is imagination? A branch of experience, expanded experience. And my experience *knows* that misfortune strikes — always — without the need of any statement by a policeman, without any statement by anyone who does not know that misfortune strikes.

You wanted to know about the house — is that good fortune, then? I didn't say so. I haven't said a word about good fortune. Misfortune is what I'm talking about. What does it always want of *us*? It wants nothing of many people; it doesn't bother about them, it rushes past. But it demands everything of some people, and they know it. Misfortune is sovereign; it lives in castles in the most miserable devil, it adorns itself with diadems in houses where there isn't a crumb of food. And those who recognize their misfortune recognize others' as well, and help to create it. Such persons ought to be locked up if they can't keep away of their own accord. They long for it.

Yes, well, but you still don't know about the house. Perhaps there's not so much to tell. It communicates on its own; perhaps it can only live as a momentary memory. Yes, precisely that: as memory, not what one remembers plus what one remembers. That will all be forgotten and sink out of sight in the thick fog. No, the memory, the assumption and expectation creating a situation together. That's what the house is like. It lives, it creates situations, God knows what it means to exist, but it *is*.

That's how it is precisely. The past and the future are of the same kind and nature. Remorse, too, is of the future. Someone who feels remorse does not act for the good, he acts for the bad, in order to have his remorse fulfilled. The house prevented this; my resident self had no wish to tempt a destiny which had shown itself to be inhospitable to excess. Does the man who has fallen into the water and been rescued with great difficulty — does he jump out into the water again immediately? Strangely enough, he does, often. To be on the safe side he sees to it that he takes his rescuer with him. Not that he wants to die. It's simply that he hasn't the gift for being rescued. I say: Let the loser remain in his defeat; he feels comfortable with it, comfortable enough for him, he's not worth a win. Some gamble for the sake of winning, some for the sake of gambling. But some simply gamble. You said something about that Theodore — after the lecture — in desperate irony: he ought to be hanged. Maybe so, I don't know his type, but maybe so. Perhaps he had merely lost his way? All right, so let him go, let him be *free*. If I had seen him I would have known. Unfortunates recognize one another by smell; birds of ill-omen fly low.'

They sat silent for a while, then he said, 'Good heavens, I was going to tell you about the House.'

'No,' she said. 'About what happened before that, what you've forgotten, you said. Why don't you tell me about that?'

'Because I *have* forgotten it.'

'Really forgotten?'

'What is forgetting? It has changed its aspect, its character — first and foremost its content. Nothing can withstand the ravages of time, nothing can withstand the narrator's tongue either. I can't tell you this about *me*, because it isn't me any longer. It was a small part of the person who had the name I've been saddled with since. To me he is "he". He was called Matias Roos, he came to be called that. His papers said so.'

She said, 'Then tell me about "him".'

'Even if he's a lie? It's so long ago.'

She placed both her hands firmly over his and said, 'He is *your* lie. Tell me what you've forgotten — about this Matias Roos.'

He said, 'Perhaps he's the one you love?'

'He's the one I love. Tell me about him.'

II

6

'My friends told me I'd get to the frontier today.'
'Which frontier?'
'The frontier. You know very well what I'm talking about.'
'All right. And who are your friends?'
'That's of no consequence.'
'Quite right. Not to us.'
'And who are "us"?'
'As we said, it's of no consequence to us.'
'I'm being as civil as I can. Who are "us"? Who *are* you?'
'And who are you?'
'You can see that from my papers.'
'A name, place of residence — what does that tell us?'
'Now look here. I've handed over these papers and had them returned, handed them over and had them returned for as far — as far back as I can remember.'
'Indeed! How far back can you remember?'

He passed his hand over his forehead. He looked into the hollow of his hand, as if the remembrance of everything might have been deposited there. He looked around him, at the long, sombre roofs of the houses stretching in a straight line as far as the eye could see in *that* direction; above the roofs, and equally sombre, the sky, lowering and slate-grey. But in the other direction, towards the frontier, or where he believed the frontier to be, the unbroken line of roofs ceased and dissolved into cheerful angles, and the sky brightened into grey-blue mist that hid everything but was also a promise: of a gap, a clearing, a change.

'Very far,' he replied at last. 'I can remember as far back as ...'

And he passed his hand over his forehead again and it occurred to him that he had no hat. He lifted his other hand and realized that it was empty too, that he hǎd no luggage. Once he had had a lot to carry; his hands had been holding so much. All of it had disappeared, little by little, both his burdens and his points of reference.

'So what is your conclusion? But it doesn't matter. You can remember far back, that's sufficient. Here are your papers.'

'But don't you want to look at them more closely — won't *all* of you look at them more closely?'

'We've looked at them.'

'And when can I get to the frontier?'

The other shrugged his shoulders. The men behind him shrugged their shoulders. As he glanced from the one to the other each man shrugged his shoulders as he looked at him. One or two of them smiled.

'We don't want your papers. Take them.'

He stretched out his hand. But whether he failed to stretch it far enough, or whether he perhaps drew it back slightly at the last moment, or whether he had been standing stupefied with disappointment and for this reason did not grasp the papers quickly enough — they fell to the pavement; the temporary passport on a loose sheet, testimonials and references which had been kept together with a rubber band, the stamped proof of identity that it had cost him years to obtain — everything fell to the ground. The wind whirled the papers into a circle, he snatched at them vainly. Suddenly they were taken by a gust and blown along the street in the direction of the frontier, or where he believed the frontier to be. He ran that way, bending down so as to grasp the papers in the air, or at least a few of them. But then the men were standing in front of him and stopped him.

'Not that way! You know that very well.'

'But my papers? The papers!'

Some of them shrugged their shoulders again.

'One must take care of one's papers. In any case you can't come this way.'

'Then send someone after the papers! Do you hear? Send someone

after my papers!'
'Calm down. Those papers are meaningless.'
'Meaningless? Do you think they are false?'
'False? No, not more so than other papers. But they're of no use to you.'
'What's the point of all this? I've been on the way for — so long! And now you've even taken my papers from me.'
'We haven't taken anything from you. The wind did it.'
'All right, the wind. But you stopped me. Your men ...'
'You can't go that way. And we didn't ask for your papers.'
'I shall have you arrested. I shall report it.'
'Are you threatening me?'
'No, no! I'm not threatening anybody. But you must understand — I am human after all.'
'What did you say you were?'
And now he could see clearly the men behind the man. The man was not smiling; he simply stood there, extremely obliging. But the men behind him were smiling; he saw the word 'human' forming itself on everyone's lips.
'I repeat that I am human. And I have the right.'
'You have the right because you are human, let's leave it at that. The right to what?'
He dropped his hands. Only now did he notice that he had been standing with them raised, that he was gesticulating with his hands in the air the way people do who have no right to anything. He realized how unconvincing he must have seemed. He recognized this situation from previous occasions, from all the times he had seen people standing in the same way, helpless, waving their arms about; people who had the right, or who once had had the right, but who increasingly forfeited their right because they could not keep their right within limits. In short: right — in relation to whom? In relation to this man who was doing his duty he clearly had no right.
'So, what is your conclusion? You had the right?'
He stood, his arms dangling. The dust from the depths of the city, from the jungle of streets and vacant lots that lay permanently covered with dust from the ruins, the dust came swirling, obscuring the visibility. And it was as if this dust clouded his very thought,

clouded his crystal-clear right — as well as the air, which had also been crystal-clear once upon a time.

'I only wanted to get to the frontier. I've travelled for a very long time, and very far.'

'That's of little consequence. Hundreds of miles perhaps? Thousands? But it's the final yards that count, the final inches — where frontiers are concerned.'

'So you think it's hopeless?'

He saw only the dust; he felt it in his mouth and his eyes.

'Why do you ask me for advice? That's an attempt at exchanging roles.'

Roles. Roles. Again this feeling that it was all a game.

'Who is a person to ask?'

And again that shrugging of the shoulders — as if a cord were joining man to man, as if they had an understanding. But they had no understanding. It was only his own words that produced this movement, that could not fail to produce it, because the question was so obviously futile.

'Is there anywhere here to spend the night?'

The man drew out two small pads from an inside pocket of his uniform. For the first time he noticed that the man was in uniform. The men behind him were in uniform as well. The man tore one ticket out of the one pad and one out of the other.

'One for lodging and one for food. Just go straight in with these.'

His voice had a certain helpfulness, almost friendliness — as when people help one another with something insignificant.

'I am much obliged to you.'

'Obliged? What does that mean?'

'I mean, I'm thanking you.'

'But why? Can't you see that you're making it appear as if I've done you a favour?'

He turned to go in. Dust clouds swept across the street. These people were wearing protective glasses against the dust; the dark lenses emphasized their anonymity. He sympathized with them. They were men who were doing their duty, without kindness it is true, but also without argument or complaint. There was a word for that: altruism. Was this altruism? Not to be continually wrapped up in one's own destiny, but to carry out one's duties one by one and so to organize the days into a progression which held a secret significance for each individual, because it had significance for the majority, for all ... But he himself felt a strong desire to express gratitude, simply to have someone to be grateful to.

'All the same, you have been very kind!'

'Let me give you a piece of advice. Stop these insinuations. There are limits to annoying an official in the course of his duty.'

There was no alternative. He went into the house. There were two shutters in the long corridor. He stood in front of one of them. It was closed. He pressed a button on the wall and the shutter sprang up. He held out his ticket.

'Other window.' The shutter crashed down. He hesitated for a moment, wondering whether there had been anyone there. Then he went to the second window. He pressed the button and the shutter sprang up. He held out the second ticket.

'First window.' The shutter crashed down.

He was left standing with the two tickets in his hand. He realized that he ought to have handed in the same ticket to window no.2 — the one that was not acceptable to window no.1. He studied the tickets. He could no longer remember which was which. He went back to window no. 1, pressed the button and held out both tickets.

'I'm very sorry ...'

One of the tickets was pushed back. Instead of the other a new ticket with five digits on it was pushed out. The shutter closed.

He took both tickets to the next window and pushed the ticket which had not been exchanged into the hatch. Instantly another ticket came out again, also with five digits on it. He glanced around him in the half darkness of the corridor; he had won a victory and considered his next move. Then he caught sight of a door at the end of the corridor. An old man was sitting on a chair to the left of it, where there was a small enclosure. From the room beyond he heard the muffled sound of plates, the faint rattle of cutlery.

He handed both tickets to the old man.

'What do I want with your sleeping pass?' said the old man crossly.

He stretched out his hand and was given back one of the tickets, whereupon he found himself in the dining hall. Some women and men were standing in a line along the wall, a plate in one hand and a spoon in the other. He looked about him, concentrating intensely, so as to avoid making mistakes. But he could not discover where these people had found their utensils. Along two bare wooden tables sat twelve persons, eating in dead silence.

The man in front of him was short, with a bald crown but collar-length hair. He was wearing a kind of uniform of striped alpaca. And now he noticed that the others were also wearing a kind of uniform, but none of them were similar. He was encouraged by the fact that they were not alike. He tapped the short man on the shoulder.

'Where do I find a plate and spoon?'

The short man half turned. He gave a quick jerk of his head backwards.

'The cupboard.'

When he turned he saw a narrow, unpainted cupboard high on the wall. He walked towards it backwards, in an attempt to move unnoticed — as if he were keeping his place in the queue. He understood his surroundings at least to the extent that he knew it didn't pay to stand out in any way. In the cupboard he indeed found spoons on one shelf and white soup plates above. With plate and spoon in his hands he slipped back into the line, which was moving slowly forward. He examined the people leaving the hatch with their plates full, to see whether they chose their seats themselves or filled up the empty ones according to some system. But he couldn't make it out. For while four or five of them had sat down in a row on the nearest empty chairs, a young woman walked, head held high, round the whole of the first table, and seated herself at the other, the one nearest the long line of uncurtained, frosted windows. He decided to do as she had done, and congratulated himself on his powers of observation.

A large woman in white was standing behind the counter, serving soup. He thanked her, and was given a hasty and embarrassed glance. He felt he should apologise for having behaved improperly, and hesitated.

'Next!'

He heard a hostile muttering from the queue behind him; then he walked, head held high like the young woman, towards the window.

'Where are you going?'

The voice from the counter was firm, but not really ill-natured. He slid into the nearest chair and put his plate in front of him with the spoon beside it, the handle at right angles to the edge of the table. He listened tensely, but the voice behind him made no objection. He thought rapidly: not at all an impossible place to be, as long as one knew how to adapt. The soup tasted good, a generous mixture of meat, vegetables and potatoes. Piles of thickly-sliced dark bread were placed down the centre of the table. He took a slice and transferred it surreptitiously to his plate. No objections from any direction. A splendid place, he thought, pleased. All you have to do is stick to the rules.

He ate slowly, partly in order to make it last longer, partly so as to observe what the others were going to do once they had finished.

Straightaway he noticed one thing: nobody was smoking, and there were no ashtrays on the table. The craving for a cigarette began long before he had finished his soup, and that caused him to eat up the rest far too quickly.

Nobody was smoking. Nobody rose from the table. Nobody spoke. Those who had finished sat looking straight in front of them, without taking the initiative to leave.

He had been fingering a cigarette from the packet in his pocket without being aware of it. The other hand was playing with his lighter.

'Have to risk it,' he muttered quietly to himself. He took out the cigarette. Those nearest him turned. He lit it quickly and inhaled four times so fast that the glow of the cigarette was reduced to a sharp point. Another pull and yet another. He waited for the protest to come like gun-shot from one direction or another, and was prepared to stub out the cigarette instantly on the rim of the soup plate.

But something else happened. All the people sitting at table, both those nearest the windows and those at the same table, turned towards him with intense expressions of interest, some of them boldly greedy, others inquisitive. A tall, dark man with hair slicked back and blue stubble on his chin threw himself across the table, quick as a bird.

'How much?' he whispered. His whole face was purple with agitation.

He handed him the packet, not out of generosity but confusion.

The man pushed the packet back again, also out of confusion. The packet with its fourteen cigarettes lay on the table between them. Everyone stared at it, except for the young woman by the window. She lit her own cigarette, but nobody paid any attention. For the first time a question formulated itself clearly in his mind: Why only my cigarettes, not hers? And the answer came quickly, automatically: Because I'm new. His hand curled greedily round the cigarette packet that he himself owned. Less than a minute ago he had owned it without reflection. Now he saw his hand as a strange hand; it curled round the packet, holding it tight. He jerked the packet towards him, and instead he took the more than half-smoked cigarette out of his mouth and handed it to the man with stubble on his chin.

The man took three or four covetous pulls and passed on the stub. It went to the next person and the next and the next. The last was an old woman with yellow cheekbones; she sucked in half a puff and ate the last crumbs of tobacco. He could see that she chewed them for a long time before swallowing them with her spittle. And his unfamiliar train of thought continued: I have power. I am in danger.

Both thoughts filled him with warmth. A situation had come about which made demands on his humanity once more. His awareness of this was mirrored immediately in his expression, giving him authority. His status had changed.

'Have you been given a room?'

'Do you prefer to have one on the top floor?'

'It's quietest up there.'

'It's easier to be further down — on the second.'

'On the first ...'

'On the third — in between ...'

'No, no, the top. Definitely the top.'

He answered, without looking up at the greedy faces, 'I'd prefer to live at the top, if I stay here. I haven't decided yet.'

This was greeted with titters from those who were sitting or standing furthest away. He had gone too far.

'If I stay here longer than the one night.'

The tittering continued. It spread to his neighbours. They took courage from having support. Only the blue man, the one who had held the packet in his hand, continued with grave determination, 'Yes, the top, the very top. I'll show you.'

They went up the stairs. The man said, 'Let me give you a piece of advice. You shouldn't say things like "If I stay here longer than the one night".'

'Why on earth not?'

'They stay here for a long time — most of them. They're a bit touchy.'

He looked at the vulgar, attractive face; it had a latent insolence about it, as did the whole person, a self-confidence that was challenging.

'I'll say what I like.'

The man with the stubble grew increasingly self-confident as they climbed. 'We should have had a lift,' he said, as if on behalf of the establishment.

'Walking's no problem, thank you.'

This show of authority irritated him. The stairs became steeper and his heart began to feel the strain. The windows in the stairwell were small, so that it was impossible to draw any conclusions about his surroundings. It was impossible to judge his unknown guide by his footsteps. He followed him, simultaneously humble and brazen, slowing his pace when *he* slowed down, increasing it when *he* went faster. Like a dog, like a shadow.

They came to a yellow corridor. There were narrow doors on either side. No sound reached them from the rooms. The man with the stubble took out a key — so perhaps he did have something to do with the place.

'Here.'

He opened the door, stepped back a little, professionally obliging. His courtesy was officious, so different from the comradely self-assertiveness downstairs over the cigarette.

'You'll like it here.'

He stood in the ridiculously small room with its ridiculous furniture. The man's remark sounded merely ironic. He took a few paces into the room and jerked himself out of the passive state of mind that was threatening to engulf him. It had begun when his papers blew away.

This is the moment to demand an explanation, he thought. The fellow owes me an explanation about this place, the way he's behaved. Besides, there's something about that face, something I remember.

But when he turned the man had gone. He closed the door and stood quite still for a long time.

7

I must sleep, I must sleep,

He lay on the narrow bed and looked up at the ceiling, closed his eyes, looked at the ceiling. It was yellow, with a sweat-brown plaster rosette left by a hanging lamp that was no longer there. He looked about him fearfully; there was no lamp anywhere, no source of light when the grey daylight was snuffed out at the window.

He closed his eyes so as to avoid seeing this fading light. He pretended that he felt sleep coming. The door opened a crack, a book was pushed in. He sprang up and seized the book. A register in a yellow paper cover. A sign of life from the management. He said, 'It seems to be a principle that everything is to happen in reverse order.' He was disappointed not to find a form with it. He had a desire to give information. Only a thick, old-fashioned visitors' register: nothing about nationality, where from, where to, purpose of stay. He longed to give all this information, to others, to himself.

So wasn't it a proper hotel? A lodging house! The room was narrow, the narrow window looked out on to the rear of a lower building. He leaned far out, but could not see the square yard below. The well was too narrow; he was too high up.

He wrote *Matias Roos*. He wrote it slowly, tensely. For the first time he had the feeling that he was giving false information when he wrote this name. This was apparently all they wanted to know, not his age, no circumstances. A name that could belong to somebody else.

He looked for a bell-push, but there was none. A narrow iron bedstead, a small table without a cloth, a chair, an old-fashioned washstand with a tin jug. He went to the door and peeped out. At once the arm was there, a hand seized the book without a word of thanks. When he walked out into the passage it was empty. No footsteps. Nor was there any sound from the other rooms further down the yellow corridor.

Supposing a person could lose all sense of who he was? After long prison sentences ... But that was not correct. During that time he had known very well who he was. It had been a reality then. The name alone had meant self-preservation. At that time.

He lay down on the bed again, looked up at the ceiling ...

By lengthy, systematic denigration of the individual: in war, behind the barbed wire in the slave camps with their policy of obliterating the personality ... but he had not been to war, nor in one of those camps ... It hadn't been like that in the big house, not at that time.

He subjected himself to the kind of cross-examination that he had expected. Where had he last come from? And before that? Whom had he met? His last meeting had been with old Buster, with Wenche and Peter Gustov. Simple enough. But it had been — in spite of all its horror, in spite of each individual's fear and loneliness — the last human meeting. Since then ...

If only he had been asked — or even better, if they had demanded that he write it down! He had done a bit of writing. It was not his profession, but at times ... If they had demanded that he write everything down, he would have been able to know everything. 'It is my weakness that things have to be written, or at any rate formulated, to acquire reality.' He silenced his voice, but not his thoughts. There was no objective knowledge of any sequence of events without their being put together into a valid form, a form which made sense of the sequence, the correct sense, not the random one. Some called it embroidering on reality. For Matias Roos it was a conjuring up of the reality of all the randomness that occurred inside him and around him.

'The rest can be filtered out.'

What could be filtered out?

The rest.

For every new period of solitariness it became more difficult for him to fight his tendency to talk to himself. More than that: to mould every situation into completed dialogue, which demanded a certain number of persons of both sexes, and of certain ages. When the situation demanded it, he increased the number of persons, but not randomly or abruptly. He moved back in his reality then and perhaps introduced the person he needed at an early stage, before he needed him, so to speak. It aroused less suspicion.

'In whom?'
'In the listeners.'
'Listeners — to what?'
'To — this, to this — who said "game"?'
'I did.'
'Oh, you. Where do you come from?'
'That's for you to decide.'
'You can't challenge me.'
'And if I do?'
'Then I shall do away with you.'
'Easier said than done.'

No, no! He groaned, he seized his head, but he was calculating the effect of the gesture; it was supposed to illustrate despair. He had to play a despairing role at having to lie like this, turning a situation which ought to demand action into unreality.

'One cannot lie for ever in a fourth-class lodging house, a down-at-heel place, not listed in Baedeker, that scarcely even exists.'
'Can't one?'
'Can't — what?'
'Lie in a lodging house ...' No, no, no, no.

He traced the simple pattern of the rosette, an S lying flat, entwined in an S lying flat, entwined in ...

'Who says one can't? Haven't you, Matias Roos, demonstrated that one can do a lot of things one is unable to do? Hasn't a long period, the whole of the latter part of your life, been spent demonstrating that one can hardly do otherwise than what one is unable to do?'
'Hold your tongue.'
'Hold your tongue yourself.'

No, no, no — I must sleep, I must sleep, I must sleep. Tomorrow

— tomorrow everything will be different.

The house was soundless. If the sounds had been there they would have disturbed him. Since they were not there, he imagined them: voices, music, words which drowned melodies, noise which obliterated the words. He imagined the gnawing of an irritating mouse somewhere in the corner behind the brown wash-stand. Just the place for a mouse to come from. He leaned out of the bed and picked up one of his shoes. He'd get that damned mouse in one throw. Or rat — of course, a rat. An almighty throw. And then: sleep — all disturbance gone.

He lay with his shoe in his hand, listening. What if somebody knocked? What if strangers came and knocked on his door, simply to pester him? In one bound he was on his feet, peering out, shoe in hand. Mouse or man — he was not going to stand for any disturbance.

He wiped the sweat from his forehead and went and lay down again — with his clothes on, as if it was clearly not his intention to sleep. Oh, Matias Roos, there are thousands of possible ways to trick oneself. But you have the advantage of knowing it, and that gives you a chance; you will trick your own trickery. You throw yourself on the bed, fully dressed, not in order to sleep, ha — who said sleep? No, in order to rest a little, stretch out for a moment after the day's — yes ... and if you should lose consciousness unwittingly, well, all the better. You're just lying there because it's not much fun sitting in a room like this. So maybe you'll sleep — without being aware of it, without being aware of it, as I said. In a short while you'll wake up and think — good heavens, you must have dropped off; now you must take your clothes off and get into bed properly. But no thank you, you know about that. If you do take your clothes off, you're finished. No, go on pretending — that's the only thing to do, but not to the extent that you're aware of it, you merely suspect, or — yes, suspect. For you can say something like: I seem to have slept away half the night; that was a really good nap, now I'll just stay here for a while. And then you'll fall asleep again until morning light. And wake up. And stretch yourself. And yawn — according to the script. And you'll say, well Matias Roos, if you didn't get some good, natural sleep that lasted the whole night! Who said I was an insomniac? That's what you'll say. Tomorrow. When you wake up. After a casual little nap that lasted the whole night ...

Instead, an army stages an invasion.

An army of images, so-called thoughts. Memory. Memory.

An army invades the head that is uppermost on this person lying here, who calls himself *Matias Roos*, I. A curious concept — both third and first persons.

And the army arrived, unannounced; no defence could prevent it. No defence was mobilized to meet the invasion. I, Matias Roos, am lying on a bed, aware that the invasion is under way with an army of memories busy as ants, linking up with new memories, sending out shoots which turn into twigs which turn into branches with leaves and flowers. Digressions, all of them digressions: deviations and preoccupations deriving from a stem which is not aware of any shoots or flowers; a stem which is bare, free of memories, solitary and without past or future and who is called Matias Roos and is lying on a bed in a lodging house for temporary guests on their way from anywhere to anywhere. I, Matias Roos, am the stem and only the stem and do not recognize one leaf and where they come from has nothing to do with me and all leaves have nothing to do with me in all their behaviour and growth: memories, plans, anxieties and reflections. For I am not even myself, but *one*, an imagined person, a nonentity, who is barely lying here, merely *is*, and barely even that. Matias Roos is an unidentified organism on its way to slumber, which *must* come, which *must* come, dear God.

A clock strikes — how many strokes? He tries to count, and at the same time to count backwards in rhythmic memorization of the first strokes he didn't manage to count. He gets to thirteen; that's too many. But the clock continues. He must have included too many from the beginning. Let's say twelve, that's the maximum for clocks. That's good, that's all right. But the clock continues with twelve more and several times twelve. It isn't a clock, but a sound born of the subconscious hope of a clock. To break into your solitude, Matias Roos, and you must face it.

He opened his eyes. There was still light from somewhere, from the window of course. And suddenly he remembered that it must be the middle of the day, or hardly that. It had been morning when he approached the frontier, when he was shown up to this room. To sleep? Why should one sleep in the middle of the day? He had walked through the night and the previous night, but what of that? Wasn't he human, with his own twenty-four hour rhythm intact?

True, he had asserted that he was human to a person, a person in uniform to be sure. That was today. He had asserted that he had certain rights on that basis, and the person had answered, 'What did you say you were?' And he had read the word 'human' on the lips of the men standing behind the one in uniform. He remembered it all now. They were the ones who had stopped him. He had been on his way somewhere, to the frontier. What frontier? The frontier. And now, as he lay here fighting against a passivity that was gradually creeping over him, he could understand that unwilling official better: a man in uniform, who had no respect for the word 'human' and for whom the word 'frontier' roused no fantasies. Naturally such an official had no clear notion of what a frontier was. It was his duty for the moment to see that nobody reached it, including himself, Matias Roos. What 'frontier' was was irrelevant to his duty. It was an abstraction. For him there was no frontier.

And as he lay on the bed, feeling passivity approaching, so familiar and so close, he himself lost the image of a frontier, the one he had created for himself — or of any frontier at all. As long as he had been on his way, as long as his expectation had flowed like sweet honey in his veins, the image had been clear.

Or had it? Peter Gustov had said, 'What do you expect of such a frontier and how do you imagine it to be?' But Peter Gustov was the type who has to diminish everything; he was a Jonah and drew others with him. More than that — defeat was his religion, he was of the dying class — no, the dying type of person, someone who only wants to do a little more damage before he falls into the abyss. That was what Peter Gustov was like, with all his affected resignation, with his talk of everything being an echo, his programme which only undermined one's courage. He had Wenche in his power — perhaps. What about himself — ? Had it not been for old Buster — *he* was the person with the ability to settle everything, all the little things, for the time being. For the time being! Absolutely no further, no lasting effect. His aimlessness after the long years in the house had led him into such company. He had lost the ultimate authority, the will to control his Self. Since then, irony had been his last defence. And irony is inverted will, no more. That was why he had left and fled.

This is treachery. The word had been in his mind when he slunk out of the flat. That had been the day after the shot in the street. The others must have heard it, but what did they do? They lied: they hadn't heard; they had lost the ability to control their own destiny. There is no other form of perdition. On the other hand it is absolute. *He* had possessed that ability — had it still, even if it only extended to flight. Wasn't that the natural way out for a single person? Not two persons, not an army of persons; their purpose is to offer one another mutual courage and possible alternatives. But when a person is alone, then flight is struggle, the only way out.

He lay, relaxed, on the bed and allowed himself to come out victorious in an imaginary discussion.

'Flight demands greater concentration than struggle. But the fugitive must know when the flight is over. That is why we flee towards frontiers, or we establish them: imaginary ones. Everyone flees towards change, towards a natural transition. From there they can look back and observe themselves. Only then can the chronology begin to take effect. Chronology? An unnatural concept! What does one remember first of all? What happened last. What is most useful to remember in order to act? What happened last. Only when you have an overview are you able to catch sight of the connections.'

As yet Matias Roos had no overview. He was lying on an iron bedstead in a house, and he did not know where it was, nor what it was. Only the march of his thoughts backwards, link by link, could clarify events for him, so that *from then on* they could become points of departure for judging his future.

He conjured Peter Gustov's voice out of the air.

'This tendency to define everything is what interferes with your urge to act. Nobody can ever be up to date; that presupposes that nothing new occurs, that time stops. Or do you expect to reach a peak of illumination?'

Yes, he did expect something of the sort, at any rate a point from which he could see himself from above, if only for a moment ...

'So you believe that life ought to appear to be organized, like some sort of painting, or a work of literature — composed?'

Yes, that's what he believed. The chemist and artist Matias Roos believed phenomena ought to manifest themselves in an orderly fashion. He believed that everything contained the possibility of a pattern.

'Like a kind of construction, a logical progression of chemical compounds, a work of art?'

'Yes, like a work of art.'

He had believed it then. He was terrified of chaos, of everything that was chaotic on a small scale: the power of the wish over objectivity, its shameful victory over the factual. That was when he had told the story of the English chair, of the life-threatening power of the imagination. And Old Buster had said, 'The wish — was it fulfilled?'

On that occasion he had not answered. Now he lay on his iron bedstead and replied,

'That's what's so terrible. It looks as if my wishes have been fulfilled. And yet it has turned out like this, a defeat in the eyes of others.'

'Which wish, in fact?'

'The wish to keep one's choices open right up to the moment when I could say, here I stand, here am *I*, that is to say, the person I am. The wish for this freedom of choice, isn't that the sum of our human worth? Instead of allowing oneself to be offered the imperative of chance, in cowardice and resignation.'

Buster, inquisitive, without irony: 'In the long run doesn't that mean letting things happen, completing one's small tasks — in other words, not choosing at all?'

Matias Roos — angry — a long time later: 'What's wrong with the fulfilled wish is that one has no idea when it is fulfilled, because our own organism presupposes expectation: expectation, the most fateful characteristic of all. For the wish is forgotten as the fulfilment gradually comes about. The wish is displaced, and appears as new wishes, simply as 'objectives'. You can't know that, you couldn't have known it on that occasion. I kept my choices open. What do *you* do? In cowardice and resignation you agree to allow yourselves to be moulded by chance, by the demands of the moment. You have never *chosen* to postpone your choice; you have simply postponed it.'

So he had reached that point again. He felt cold. There was always a moment when his own company became intolerable. Then he went looking for anything, no matter what; and that was what interfered with everything, that was when things happened, chance occurrences, these lengthy conversations about nothing, which introduced new topics into a picture which demanded clarification; then it took longer and longer to reach a stand-still, an overview.

Outside it was raining quietly. He heard the rain as a dull swishing against the walls and the base of the shaft. It made him feel lonely and shut in. With one bound he got up from the bed and stood in the middle of the floor, trembling with indecision. He must investigate this house, must find some of the people in it. He walked towards the door but stopped short of turning the handle.

Was this exactly what he should not be doing? Wasn't he about to take just the kind of insignificant action that would spoil his chance of an overview? There was a saying about letting the situation ripen. He said, 'The situation must be allowed to ripen.'

But — and as often previously — he pushed the thought aside. He simply could not bear to be alone any longer. He was too weak a vessel to withstand the temptation to know, to let things happen, even though they might give rise to disaster.

'I provoke disaster. I'm the person who's to blame for ...'

He stood in the middle of the room holding his head, as if to test its physical weight against unfortunate decisions.

'I'm to blame for what happens.'

His own words made him shudder. He went over to the mirror above the wash-basin. It was a mirror advertisement for margarine. It reflected his face as if seen through water. The nursery rhyme came into his head, in distorted form: Little mirror that I spy, Can you tell me, who am I? And as he formulated the idiotic verse, the mouth in the mirror twisted into a derisive sneer. It was reminiscent of Peter Gustov. He turned back to the room and let all deliberation die away and said aloud, 'Another illusion. To manufacture an "impulse"!'

The next moment he had his shoes on.

'I've put on my shoes. I've tied the laces. I've let it happen unconsciously, so as to surprise myself with a decision.'

Then he was standing in the yellow corridor, and was filled once again with the urge to act, to be decisive. It was now of enormous importance to him to tiptoe past the narrow doors without being seen. He was filled with a boyish delight at breaking the rules. They showed you your room, and you were supposed to stay there. Once he had lived in a large house with a lot of rules. 'Idiocy!' he said.

The corridor curved and ended in a small window which gave so much light, it must have looked out on to an open space. He saw the rain in stripes on the pane and heard it swishing in the air, or against trees. For a moment the sound preoccupied him completely: the swish of rain in the treetops. He suddenly felt secure and at ease.

Before him stood a man in a white jacket. Both of them halted. The stranger looked at him enquiringly.

'I'm going to take a walk round the house,' said Matias Roos. He could have bitten his tongue off. Was he going to make excuses to a person in a white jacket?

'As you wish. The bar is downstairs, this way.'

'I'm not going to the bar — and if you mean that chilly café with the unpainted tables, I've been there already.'

'You haven't been to the bar. I had the honour of showing you upstairs from the café. You were so kind as to offer me a cigarette.'

Now he remembered the blue stubble; it was less blue now. The man had changed into a waiter's uniform. So he was on the staff, someone he almost knew.

'Forgive me, I didn't recognize you at first.'

'Not so easy. I'm in my uniform now. They call me Daniel, the Auxiliary.'

'Haven't I met you before?'

'You were so kind as to offer me a cigarette.'

This monotonous repetition of his kindness seemed like a provocation. Matias Roos looked at the man steadily. 'I meant ...'

But the man's glance slid away. His compliant courtesy hardened into a brick wall. Past occasions danced through his brain. He had to find out, find out, find out. There was a paralysis in the air; he refused to give in to it.

'Do look round the house, ' smiled the Auxiliary, blocking his path. 'The way to the bar ...'

'I've told you I'm not going to any bar.'

' ... to the bar — !' The man gestured with his hand. The transverse passage ended in an arch.

'Down those stairs ... ' And with the smile a new and curious thought occurred to Matias Roos. Yes, I *have* met him before — in a different version.

The stairs were carpeted, deadening the sound of footsteps. As soon as he stepped under the low arch he encountered a different world. Yet again he was astonished that in the same moment he could scarcely remember what it had been like a short while ago: the narrow room with the iron bedstead, the corridor with the yellow walls, the cold light at the end of the passage. On the staircase everything was red and warm. And the thought occurred to him again: when everything is suddenly changed, am I then the same? Is a person's identity as immutable as we like to believe?

He heard the faint notes of a flute, a touching little melody, very simple. Again a change — just through a simple melody played on a flute? I'll shake it off, I want to reach a definite point. But he continued downwards. The stairs spiralled lower and lower, always soundless, with only a weak light from a lamp on each landing. The tones of the flute became louder, but the melody was the same. And in that moment the memory came to him of the friends he had left. Now he knew it had been long ago. This had been no sudden flight; it had been a long journey — oh, so long. He was tired and thirsty and felt as if he had come a long way. It had been a great kindness on the part of this Auxiliary — so modest to let himself be called that — a kindness to show him the way to the bar like this. He might meet people there, have a drink. At once he felt cheerful. It was natural, too, that the stairs should extend so far down; his room was high up, and bars were usually placed at the bottom, often below ground level. The notes of the flute were coming closer and closer. He began the internal dialogue which consoled him so often.

'Well, well, this suits me nicely.'

'Whom does it suit?'

'Me.'

'Oh?' And Buster's voice: 'One thing follows another!'

'I say it suits me nicely. *Me.*'

He walked downwards, humming. He was not running away from anyone who was asking him questions. It would suit him to meet some people now. A bite of food and a glass of something would be pleasant. He could hear the clink of glasses already. And an axe chopping — no mistaking that sound — it was a meat axe, cutting up chops. He smelt the fragrance of grilled meat. He congratulated himself, and thought, you're congratulating yourself. You're acting as if you're pleased.

'I *am* pleased,' he said aloud.

'Or acting as if you are.'

'I am!'

He repeated the words in order to soften the effect of something unusual. Always objections from every direction when one was at last pleased about something, unworthy objections. 'Who's worthy?' 'Me. One doesn't have to accept all kinds of opposition, not people who lie in wait and attack verbally. I'm thinking of Daniel, the Auxiliary — a pleasant fellow!'

'But with an ingratiating smile.'

'Ingratiating! That's the sort of thing people say. One must get to know people; they improve on acquaintance.'

'And if one learns to know them even better, they acquire a curious ability to become precisely how they were the first time one saw them.'

'This faith in first impressions is ridiculous. Intuition, I suppose? One can't ...'

Now he could hear the flute very close. It met him all of a sudden at a curve in the staircase where he found himself on the level. From this point the passage led straight forward. There was a door with leaded panes. A nice, old-fashioned bar. He said so aloud, confirming the fact: 'A nice, old-fashioned bar.'

And now no evil voices in him replied. He had arrived.

There was a flap in the door. He peered through it cautiously into semi-darkness. At the same moment a face appeared in front of him on the other side of the flap, smiling agreeably. Then it was gone. Matias Roos closed the flap and smoothed his hair. All previous moments suddenly vanished on the instant, as if nothing had ever happened previously. He put his hand on the latch, and pressed it down slowly.

'He's coming,' said a voice quietly, close to the door.

Every time I cross the frontier to a fortuitous circumstance, a fresh ... It was at this precise moment — as he touched the iron latch of the heavy door and at the sound of the voice which said, 'He's coming' — at that moment he remembered something of bygone days.

Bygone days. The phrase itself, with its smell of mildew, merely told him that it was a long time ago. He remembered the company of his friends and the reason why he had drifted away from them. Small parts of a whole were revealed to him, so that he was forced to think: each time I cross the frontier to a fresh, fortuitous circumstance it is immediately too late to see clearly. Then everything must happen. What is happening now is unavoidable, but decisive as well. These moments always occur in such a way that in the same second and for the same reason as the past tries to organize itself, I must enter on something new, which wipes it all out once more. But in this second I remember, and know, a part of what happened last time.

We were sitting beside the radio, waiting for a shot, an explosion. We had put the life of an unhinged nonentity at risk to test my invention somewhere down the street, and the shot went off and it was believed to be a random political attack. And God in heaven knows it was random, as random as what it was aimed at, as are all politics which greet all miscalculations with an omniscient smile — What did we tell you? — and which change course and pretend it happened just as predicted. A random attack on randomness, a whim, an experimental attack on lack of imagination and bungling and omniscience after the event; that was the essence of this kind of politics, which disconcerted honest people, so that they thought they themselves were stupid.

Afterwards he had fled.

Afterwards he had been a wanted man.

Afterwards it was *he* who had been guilty. Wanted persons are guilty.

What irony! Always guilty of the few things he hadn't really ... But in general. In general!

Afterwards it became known that he had been away for a long time once before and had lived in the large, secure house, so secure that he had forgotten that there was perhaps a world called the outside.

Afterwards: flight. And after that: the frontier. Frontiers are tempting; the frontier is security between the deed and the man. Beyond it anything can happen, perhaps something new.

And in that second Daniel's face appeared in front of him too. The Auxiliary from the corridor.

'Bertram!'

'There you are! Didn't I say he had an ingratiating smile?'

Everything in this single moment — as if the whole of his life had been moments. Everything else: nothing. Another moment: the English chair ...

He knew all this — I, Matias Roos.

But it was too late in this all-inclusive moment, too late to remember. Something new was added. A powerful *that time* ... It passed quickly through his brain as he laid his hand on the latch, in the moment when a voice said, 'He's coming.'

8

Matias Roos was sitting in the darkest corner when the shot was fired.

He was sitting with his face turned towards the radio. It was so dark that the half moon of the dial was clearly illuminated. The tuning eye stared at him evilly with its column of half-light. The column expanded and contracted a little, like the pupil of a real eye; it hypnotized him.

The shot rang out distantly. Several blocks away. He listened with his back, to see whether the others had heard it. Their endless conversation continued, monotonous and muffled, as it had for some days. He, who had been listening to the radio, was the only one who had heard it.

As far back as he could remember he had sat leaning over the radio — only light and many shifting sounds: music, farming reports, news, news, news, the same news from all directions. From time to time he moved the right hand knob to find a different sound to be distracted by.

He was filled with an internal chill after drunkenness, with a despair that renewed itself in waves. The wave came, he bent double, as if he were standing on deck, flexing his knees against the swell.

Better to sleep — but he dared not, dared not wake up again, not even when sleep was near. He should have seized the chance, but the blessed opportunity to fall asleep had been lost. He closed his eyes, daggers of light danced behind his eyelids, the low sounds and melodies of the radio became screams. The radio provided a consoling check on the state of being awake. From its hypnotic stare pictures arose, from its voices other voices arose, events from far back in time. What voices and melodies are embedded in a person? What common denominator unites them, and links them with the self? They did not concern him, neither voices nor melodies, but they were there, everything from the past repeating itself. Even the sound of a shot that he had been waiting for did not penetrate this memory-wall of unimportant things, this reality which had established itself against his will, even against his true receptivity. For how long? For as long as *it* wished, this reality, for an 'always' which must have arisen from minute to minute in conditions of defencelessness which threatened to become an 'always'.

After this unexpected 'always'?

Nothing. New voices, new indifference against which one could not defend oneself.

All this time he could hear the voices, three layers of voices: the voices from the past, which arose from the voices in the radio; the voices in the living room behind his back. Tolerant voices, those behind him, phlegmatic and incessant like the voices of people when they have spent a long time together and all topics are exhausted, so that only the silence is left to be talked away. They must have heard the shot?

Bernhard's sonorous voice, and Peter Gustov's with its wearisome repetition, and Wenche's high pitch, piping and unattractive and featureless. And Old Buster's infrequent bass, incredibly deep; concise and melodious each time it intervened after long intervals. It resembled the double bass which joins in on every tenth sheet of the score with only three or four strokes of the bow. And yet it was Old Buster's bass that gave shape and meaning to the melody.

The words said nothing to him any longer. It was all echo. That was why the distant shot remained suspended emptily in the space where it should have been the only voice.

Matias Roos looked at his watch from time to time, immediately forgetting what it had told him. He wanted to know now: a quarter past three. Night or day? He pondered for a long time. Day. The same day as ... A foggy, mild winter's day with the blinds drawn down. A sharp pain shot through him at this confrontation with a reality within the one he had created for himself out of voices. He gathered all his strength in order to chase the moment away, so that it should not eat into those areas which were the land he had promised himself, an 'always'.

Hands and feet like ice, his head burning. It shaped itself, as usual, into something that could be hummed under his breath: 'With feet at the Pole and hell-fire at his head ...'

He could hear the shot when he wished. But had he heard it? He listened. No shot. So it had occurred. For when he had heard it he had not been listening, so he had not imagined it.

Once upon a time the mornings had been carefree!

There had been mornings without any relapse into thoughts filled with horror, mornings with choice, with days of work ahead, free of danger. Happy mornings for anyone who wished himself and others well. And before *that*? And before *that*! There was always a 'before that' which cropped up and attempted to give meaning to something closer. Like the first time he met the General ...

The old General who lived in a goatshed and ate reindeer lichen and trout all summer — to cleanse himself of civilization. Had he been a general? His voice came to him:

'Young man, you are nourishing a viper in your bosom.'

'What viper, Buster?'

(Yes, of course — it was Buster, Old Buster as they were calling him already, who was sitting in the living room now, growling something at long intervals — the same person, both him and *him*.)

'Your own destroyer, young man.'

They were smoking fish on that occasion. They had been sitting in a stone hut, smoking trout all day long, so that the smoke was making their eyes smart fit to fall out of their heads, and they had the smell of juniper in their hair and clothes until far into the autumn.

'And how shall we drive out this enemy, Wise Old Man?'

(Oh, how young and jocular one was once upon a time, using such uninhibited slang!)

'In Finland they get worms from eating fresh-water fish raw. Then they take a cure that's so drastic, it's pure chance who survives, the patient or the worm.'

'Oh Wise Man — and what is the name of the worm in my case?'

'You share the same name.'

'And who is to drive out whom, Wise Man — who will survive?'

Old Buster — what could he have answered? That was fourteen years before the shot, and Buster was Old Buster then as now, a permanent fixture in one of the old insurance companies in the centre of town, of the type the customers met in morning dress and shining black shoes, oh so polished! In summer he lived in the goatshed and wore a goatskin jacket with the hair on the outside, and bathed in ice-cold mountain tarns on those shining mornings with a wisp of mist above the mirror-surface of the water; and then his body was clothed in grey hair too, his own grey hair, a natural wild man's pelt which he hid beneath the morning dress in daily life ... Yes, he had replied, 'Your parasitical destroyer is identical with the young person we know and cherish, son of the old man, son of an immigrant with an instinct for his own good.'

'And did you know these people, Buster? It sounds like pre-history.'

'Everything's relative. I never set about judging a person without the help of a couple of generations. Only through the grandparents does one begin to perceive a person's shape.'

'What about my father?'

He had asked with a certain tension, even in that period of carefree youth.

'He was far from being as unambiguous as the old man. He had already begun to lack that natural instinct for what's up and what's down.'

'Which I lack completely, I suppose?'

'Which you overlook. Your parents moved around in various countries. You were born at a customs post.'

That same Buster, in this living room. And Wenche — the lady from that summer at the hotel. What does 'the same' mean?

And those who had joined them? Peter Gustov — and perhaps he still felt as if a cold cloud passed over a landscape in sunshine when the name came up ... And Bernhard. They were all there, they were the same persons, and it was in the same life, in which all elements change place and nevertheless lay claim to amount to the same sum.

He sat in front of the radio in that darkened room, knowing it. But he could not understand it. At some point something must have been capable of change! It must be possible to halt or divert a movement. Perhaps all the moments that he had labelled 'too late' had been precisely the right moments, perhaps even up to the moment labelled 'now'; any kind of moment, for instance, the one when the shot was fired.

But this thought never reached the surface until it *was* too late. Nor the thought that the same people were 'the same'. Each one of them functioned as the next stage of the person who had met 'the others' that summer.

That was the summer they had called the carefree summer. One question was in the air: what does it mean to be carefree? At the moment of definition it has gone. They had given it that name; it was the role of that summer, as décor. So it had been carefree, a kind of release, the release of one individual, helped by another. They had passed some time at a country hotel, each one of them under the umbrella of his pretext. He himself, because he was convalescing after a humiliating period which had taxed his spirits beyond all reason, and forfeited the self-respect which is the reflection of the respect of others. The General and insurance agent ('Heaven knows whether *he's* ever been a General!') because he was the hotelier's adviser and had arranged the transfer of the hotel to a share company: this Buster could be the friend of two parties without being false towards either of them. Wenche and Bernhard because they could not take a holiday together officially as long as she was waiting for her divorce. Peter Gustov because he was one of those lone wolves who appear from nowhere and become the focus of attention with the aid of their unreliable charm; besides, he was studying hotel management in order to invest some of his extensive wealth. None of them felt any attachment to the others except for their need to distance themselves from the other guests. Nor were they in the habit of going early to roost; that is a characteristic which links strangers together into a fellowship which starts in the bar and ends with their going for walks together without any prior agreement.

Peter Gustov received many letters, a whole pile every lunch time. He would open them over the coffee, slowly and without interest, which increased the curiosity of others. One day he remarked, 'This Wenche must hold the record for brief marriages.'

Matias Roos followed the direction of his tired glance, over to the table where the young couple had just got to their feet. Matias Roos did not like the comment. All the same — oh, such damned politeness! — he leaned forward.

'One day. Exactly twenty-four hours. A morning wedding on the Friday, divorce proceedings Saturday noon.'

Matias Roos got to his feet. The young couple came in front of him in the revolving door. Outside the summer day was sparkling, newborn after a shower of rain. Leaves glittered, the gravel paths were dark with moisture. Everything indoors in the glassed-in dining room suddenly felt stifling. This Peter Gustov who sat finding out about things ... He put him out of his mind, but ideas are contagious, and later — when he saw Wenche sitting on her yellow bench beside the tennis court, waiting for Bernhard — he thought, what in the world could have happened in the course of one day like that? Is the experience of that one day the reason for the thin veneer of cynicism that surrounds even her kindest actions: a thin but permanent veneer, like an artificial sheen on the surface of all this beauty, her slightly too cheerful beauty? Her smile coming a little too quickly, as if ordered a little in advance, and lasting just a little too briefly to convey genuine warmth: this phenomenon that none of us fails to notice even though we never remark on it, and which looks as if it suits handsome young Bernhard so splendidly that it would almost be an insult to *his* layer of veneer if the warmth had been genuine and the charm less conscious?

Matias Roos had gone over to her then, in a confused impulse to — perhaps to console her. The gravel crunched, she looked up with an expression of ... (and this same expression appeared at this moment of decision while he stood at the threshold of a transition in his life, at the threshold of a bar —) there was fear in her expression. Anything else? An icy coldness. It altered quickly. Only the nervous seeker after states of mind could have detected the transition. It altered to that graciousness which made her the little leading lady of the place, a ray of sunshine in which everyone bathed, with the same kind of optimism as when holiday-makers call it sunshine if the sun *is* there, behind a film of cloud. At that moment he had called her the cellophane girl and abandoned the role of consoler. 'Bernhard will be here soon,' he said. And she: 'Why do you say that?' He: 'Because I play in all comedies with the best of intentions.' And she, a little surprised, perhaps *almost* happy: 'Then I've understood you correctly.'

Then Bernhard had appeared, light brown hair, athletic, slight — the very picture of a man. The picture ... Matias Roos, under his breath: 'Understood me correctly in what?' She, hastily and with the shadow of a smile: 'In that you, too, perceive matters only as reflections of things.'

They had known something about one another then. So Peter Gustov had most likely received letters about himself as well: letters about his suspicious absence from respectable society, that society which notices those who are absent. Matias Roos sat down and let the young couple go for their walk. High up in the diving tower above the swimming pool he saw Peter Gustov, running to fat, in bathing trunks, heavy and Buddha-like, with small eyes behind his glasses, watching the three of them down in the grounds with lazy attention. At the same moment as he knew he had been observed he made a gesture of invitation, as if to say: Come up here and share my nervousness at being unable to dive from a height I've worked up to against my will.

They had talked about this: that one placed oneself in situations and then dared not take the consequences. Mountain peaks, examinations, provoked danger, initiated misdeeds. The delight — or at any rate the pleasure — of placing oneself in a risky situation and then — being 'saved'. All of it in order to increase the joy of life? To discover it! Peter Gustov had said, 'We're voluntary artistes in the circus.' He said such banalities with a calmness that was scornful in itself; anyone who acknowledged his platitudes out of goodwill was himself put to shame on account of his provoked politeness.

Small sparks between aimless holiday makers — cold sparks which gave out a little light but set fire to nothing, between the one play-actor and the other ... He had stood in the gravelled space, looking up at that amiable grimace in a face which refused to express anything other than a grimace. He had stood feeling a secret pleasure at what is false and dangerous.

Something real did happen, one of those events which began to link them together. The man they called the General was found more dead than alive up in the sinister Tarn, caught in a fishing net. Some farmers had intended to put out the net that afternoon, but it had not been hanging on the wall of the little boathouse. They were going to set it out in the tarn instead of hauling it. They all talked at once, they were telling the truth: 'Old Buster' must have positioned the net there himself. Peter Gustov remarked in the bar that evening: 'The only general to be caught in a net ... He has a wife, by the way, with a flat in the Avenue Wagram. She has only one breast.' Nothing more, just enough to speculate on, if anyone was interested.

Wenche, with one of her enchanting, fleeting smiles, said, 'What in the world brings people like us together? It must be that we're not inquisitive. It makes it easier to guess about each other.'

When they put two and two together it turned out that the General had had a phone call from abroad that morning. That sort of thing does not escape attention. Someone calls out that it's long distance, everything is set in motion. When General Buster came out of the telephone box in the lobby his face was grey. He immediately commented on the weather and gave advice about mosquito bites; he asked strangers how they had slept last night — 'besides, not all mosquitoes bite, only the female, never the male, it can't, the female is a bloodsucker'. He helped the gardener to use the roller on the tennis court and joined the people emptying the swimming pool; somebody had complained about the state of the water. 'In America they did it like that.'

This was in the morning. After lunch he went for a walk. No, he would prefer to go alone, then one could enjoy nature best, decide one's own pace, alter the route if one felt so inclined. He talked to several people about the advantages of this. He was going to follow the course of the stream downhill towards the forest and then perhaps catch the bus on the main road.

An hour later Peter Gustov said, 'The General turned back when he reached the bottom of the slope. He went uphill towards the mountain. He looked as if he was making for the Tarn.'

Nobody thought any more about it then, except perhaps that this

Peter Gustov was a dab hand at keeping an eye on everyone — a strange interest, finding out what people really did and really thought, as if it was important to unmask one another. Later, when resuscitation was over and the old man had been taken to his room in the south wing to rest, then one or two people did look askance at Peter Gustov. He acted as if he had known all along.

It could be uncomfortable. It had once had an uncomfortable effect on him, Matias Roos. A few of the guests had been sitting together, and they arrived at the conclusion that such places are strange: the first week passes incredibly slowly, but the next has gone before you can turn round. People made remarks like that. People had sat together at such places and remarked on it so often that the trees mimicked it ironically in the night wind. Peter Gustov said, 'That's how it is with time — as always under unusual conditions which become usual. I've been told that prisoners lose their sense of time; they can't manage to keep track of whether two or, for instance, three and a half years have passed.'

He had not looked at Matias Roos then. He had so obviously not looked at him that Matias Roos decided he definitely had grounds for not having heard the remark. So he had said, 'You can hear things astonishingly clearly in the country. Last night I could hear the train from right down in the valley, even though I wasn't listening for it.'

People sit at leisure, making such remarks. It hurts nobody. And yet such unimportant words can contain dagger thrusts, as when Peter Gustov replied, 'As we were saying ...!'

... and everyone laughed. People are appreciative, sitting round a trolley with coffee, three kinds of cake, and small, gilded liqueur glasses which glimmer ruby red in the afternoon sun. Then they look for a long time at the glass with its thick, sugary streaks moving slowly downwards from the rim. You sit in the sun, an individual together with another individual, playing that you are in company. It's called the being-together-game, it's called the aren't-we-enjoying-ourselves-game, and it is played by those who are trying to wrest a point in the struggle against loneliness, if only for half an hour over the coffee — until someone appears to take a quick decision, stifles a yawn, and suggests that a little nap really might be rather pleasant. And the only person to be fooled is the person who believes he is fooling everyone else, and all of them know that from now on he is taking up the burden of his loneliness again, because it could not be kept at a distance after all. And the person who is left sitting without taking any initiative will be odd man out and will have to pretend to be enjoying the view.

It is in this creeping panic, when a person's stay is coming to an end, that someone makes the unfortunate proposal that they really ought to meet in town some time, and it is this proposal which gets far too enthusiastic support, because the lack of it would be absolutely outrageous, and perhaps each individual has in fact been thinking along the same lines and is glad because he hasn't mentioned it himself, for the person who did is odd man out again.

So it seems to be under those circumstances that those who do *not* say such things join forces without wishing to do so. One evening in the bar you may blurt out a confidence of some sort, much against your will. Or a fresh, dewy morning invites enraptured inconsistency while waiting for fried egg and bacon. All it takes is that you should differ from the imaginary average who are called other people.

So, they seek each other's company. Not that they've been looking .... People seek each other out who have no more in common than a certain urge to belittle, in self-defence. ('Perhaps the man is predisposed towards disappointment?') The time for heartfelt approaches has arrived ('because he's afraid of something — ?') This is how such approaches are made.

The diffident, handsome Bernhard to Matias Roos one dull, grey day up on the peaked knoll behind the hotel: 'You've been very kind during our stay. My fiancée and I appreciate it. I've heard so much about your splendid inventions — a long time ago ...'

Matias Roos to Old Buster, the General, as they tighten the net on the tennis court: 'From the very first, a long time ago, you taught me a great deal about myself. That time we smoked fish in the mountains ...'

The General, on his part, to young Wenche of the glazed features: 'I have faith in love! When I see a young couple like yourself and Bernhard I tell myself: the wish to defend oneself, and love, that's what I have faith in, no matter what experience life offers. Call me Buster ...'

Wenche to Peter Gustov: 'I don't understand how you manage to see right through people like that. But I can tell you *one* thing: *I'm* happy. Happy, do you hear?'

(And that was on the bench, the one that had become her bench rather than anyone else's, to such a degree that you got to your feet stealthily shortly after she had sat down with her mask of beauty.)

Finally Peter Gustov to Matias Roos: 'They're all like children; they're children, they can be made to take an interest in anything — a serious game. There's something I want to say to you, by the way. If you need any money to continue with your experiments ...'

'Experiments?'

' ... I have a little spare capital. Tell me, don't you miss that kind of capital any more — I mean those people who finance such things?'

'I don't understand you.'

'And yet you do understand me. You didn't react in the slightest when I mentioned that you'd been in prison. Good Lord, it was between ourselves, after all. But those people who — well, who betrayed you, that man who let you suffer for it ...'

'I've forgotten such matters.'

'Oh no. One doesn't forget, one represses it, the sum of insult accrues, it grows and grows. With what right, you ask, do I, a stranger, remind you of unpleasant matters? In the first place I'm not asking about right, no more do you; right is an attitude. But those men who financed you once, that man above all who sacrificed you "for the sake of the greater good" — his invisible presence is here, after all ... no, no, not for the others, they're children, but for you, and in part for me as well.'

'You're right. I *could* know what — who — you're talking about. But I don't wish to. What's past is past.'

'Yet it isn't, as I said. If anything isn't past, it's this past. He's not past, the Financier. He's not here, you'll say. You harbour no bitter feelings, as one says when one does harbour bitter feelings. The thought of revenge — '

'Certainly not revenge. There you're mistaken.'

'Very well. But you were an employee, a dependent. You were highly paid in order that you should feel independent, but you were the more dependent because of it. When the stakes became too high somebody had to be sacrificed. You.'

'The person to whom you refer is not here, as you so rightly remark.'

'And I remark even more rightly, he *is* here, he'll always appear wherever you are, he'll be standing beside your bed when you wake — a symbol, perhaps. One day you'll meet him in the flesh.'

'My feelings of resignation matured a long time ago.'

'Or almost did so. Everything reappears. Everyone. I said that in the first place I was not asking for the right to interfere in your affairs. In the second I speak as your friend. Inactivity, let me tell you, will not suit you in the long run.'

'It's best for those who are unfortunate to remain inactive.'

'As your friend, as I said. Come and see me in town. I don't understand much about destructive technology, but destruction *per se* interests me. We're certainly the only persons here who are adult.'

... And all of it with that winning smile which could suddenly dispel antipathy. Matias Roos did not hate this perspicacious person. His smile negated his impertinence. Who was it who talked about 'the meeting of souls'?

Well, that was meant ironically. But that was how everything began between these casual acquaintances, because they were in a sense washed up, each one of them. And Matias Roos was capable of being aware of it, with all his ability, which he cursed, to be aware of everything in brief moments, moments which occurred when he found himself at the threshold of change — at the moment, for instance, when a voice had said, 'He's coming.'

9

They had called themselves The Destroyers. They formed a club; they went on playing the summer game indoors. Anyone could put what he liked into the game, whatever amused him.

The General, for instance. All of a sudden he seemed to have lost his good nature. In all seriousness he wanted to nominate his friends to a circle of fanatics, who were to provoke, by acts of terrorism, the will of the nation to defend itself. Throughout his long life he had spoken about politics with a smooth tolerance; now he was playing the soldier. The insurance agent had once been a captain in the reserve. He had been hiding a dream; he was quite simply a warmonger. (Peter Gustov: 'A kind of extended infantilism that has not expressed itself previously. It's like developing a film.')

And Wenche, who could say to the General with a blank expression (Peter Gustov: 'She hasn't a single expression that a wrinkle can grow out of'): 'You're so sweet when you're manly, Buster. I think society needs people like you. People nowadays can't be aroused without gun-fire.'

The General did not boast then; he didn't dare, because she made him uncertain. They were at Peter Gustov's house. They were always there. He was rich and he was a bachelor. Their host said, 'You don't often meet beautiful women who are intelligent.' And when he said that kind of thing he looked steadily at Wenche, in order to compromise her with yet another banality. She replied, 'Or rich men who are so unpleasant. Most of the rich apologise for themselves these days.'

Then handsome Bernhard was uneasy and had to interrupt,

usually with an experience when out shooting, about how a grouse had behaved once in an extraordinary way at a certain place. Nobody moved while he stumbled through his shoot, his vacuous nonsense. 'Never seen a grouse to equal it!' Wenche raised her glass to him and remarked to the General, 'The movement needs the young men, Buster.'

And Buster chuckled his gratitude. Her understanding of military preparedness impressed him strongly. An old romantic who had known the women and men of his generation from the upper crust, his enthusiasm was an echo of a former enthusiasm, evoked by a cellophane girl.

And was not he himself, Matias Roos, flattered, or at the very least, relieved? This Peter Gustov was an amiable person, dealing in business for pleasure. He made money on a board game for adults and children, 'The Little Mathematician'. He had seen something in a shop window as he passed and set Matias Roos to improving it ('I assume you're an expert on board games; one learns that kind of thing to perfection in our humane institutions'). It was a board game based on the curious behaviour of certain primary numbers in a wider context. The game caught on like wild-fire throughout the country. People challenged one another in deadly earnest and the results were reported by the radio beyond national borders. ('If you had invented such a game on your own it would have been called a pastime; it would have been sold at Christmas-time in batches of five hundred. Now it's an important contribution to adult education. The man who invented chess talked a lot of nonsense about grains of wheat. You'll get five thousand, so I don't suppose it matters to you what I get out of it?')

He was right. Matias Roos was completely indifferent to what Peter Gustov got out of it. This slightly comic lazybones with his insatiable curiosity about his fellow human beings also busied himself with naive inventions for the purpose of destruction, such as exploding fountain pens. He talked about ultrasound which could disturb the human organism to the point of death. In Matias Roos's laboratory they experimented with the members of the club, causing them to vomit and bleed from the eyes and throat. Nobody protested. They were playing at science and discussed with scholarly zeal how much significance these experiments might have for the world.

Yes, Peter Gustov was an amiable man, a man who was not working towards any discernible goal, one of the few whose wealth caused him grief and who wanted to use it to give pleasure to others. Besides, they were given the small pleasure of being dominated. They liked it, and when it occurred to them that they disliked it they liked that as well; it was pleasant to pursue their desire for freedom on a small scale. They, too, were filled with this comfortable compulsion to ignore everything that had seemed important, in order to be able to concentrate all the more conscientiously on inveterate sociability — a goal in itself. But Peter Gustov was circumspect over food and drink; his tendency to put on weight excused a host's moderation in everything except the observation of others and permitting them to squirm for their own delight.

This was the being-friends-game in a club which maintained certain formalities. Peter Gustov had an unusual collection of weapons, modern and antique, and it was his invariable demand that his friends should practise their skills in the use of firearms on the built-in terrace, one wall of which was reinforced. They fired at targets with ancient blunderbusses and modern pistols. They shot before and after meals, in order to measure the effect of alcohol on their precision. It amused him to watch others' reactions to weapons. Matias Roos, for example, who once upon a time had constructed intricate explosives in the service of a military power, never became familiar with the use of an ordinary Colt. 'You hold it as if you were afraid of it. Look at that young lady. When she shoots she never misses a chance. She shoots to kill.'

And it was striking for all to see how Wenche lost her indifference completely when she was holding a weapon in her hand. And they all suited her: the foil, which she wielded with virtuosity, or the heavy military pistol. She extinguished seven lights in the solid silver candelabra with seven shots and was rewarded with a drink from the Gustov family's Persian goblet. She was perhaps the only one of them who compelled their host's interest in this respect.

Not one of them was at the scene when the shot was fired. They had spent a good deal of time together, and knew what was going on.

The newspapers called it an act of political vandalism that might have started a world-wide conflagration. Some people thought there were forces behind it whose purpose was to shock, a group of perverted idealists who wanted to rouse an apathetic public. All agreed that something was afoot and that illuminated objects were moving across the sky at night. A caretaker in a small town had heard a whistling sound when he was out seeing to the chickens. A deaf-mute carrying two grenade-like objects was arrested. His impenetrable naiveté suggested that he was under the influence of hypnosis. The police worked according to an accepted method: which persons were at liberty?

Matias Roos was sitting in the darkest corner of the living-room when he heard the shot. He sat hunched over, his face turned towards the radio, staring into the dim, magic eye that resembled the sleepless, malicious eye of a chicken. The dial shone dully into the room.

Peter Gustov had risen to his feet. He had laid aside his spectacles as he listened, *after* the shot. Now he was fumbling on the table, feeling for his glasses before he saw them. His face was unrecognisable until he put them on; then it became commanding. Slowly he walked across the carpet and stood with the bookshelves behind him, while the conversation continued on the other side of the room.

'Well?'

Matias Roos stood up without taking his leave. He left, knowing that it was the last time, and that they had no reason to reproach him. But they knew that the moment he left they were free. They knew that wanted persons are the guilty ones.

Peter Gustov followed him out into the hall.

'It will take you a week to get to the frontier.'

'Which frontier?'

'That's your choice.'

'You mean a real frontier? The frontier — ?'

They stood in the half light of the hall. Peter Gustov went to the filing cabinet and took out a pile of banknotes.

'I'll give you two addresses, then you'll get all the papers you need. The money has been saved from what's owing to you. No need to thank me.'

Matias Roos read the addresses carefully, tore up the slips of paper, and burned them in the ashtray. Peter Gustov nodded his approval.

'Which frontier?' he repeated. 'You and I are not children.'

He made an almost invisible gesture with his head towards the living room.

'When we play, we play in earnest, that is to say, according to our nature. Can you or any one else complain if it's dangerous?'

Matias Roos held out his hand but Peter Gustov took no notice. He said, 'You have in fact been very close to the frontier, to the limit, ever since we met. Believe me, I recognize a person who's sleepwalking.'

10

To sum up:
He is fleeing. Not to, only from. Not simply from what happened last; the last is always a pretext. He is an inventor, perhaps an artist. Who has invented him? Important men invent him every time he can be put to use. He is fleeing from the important men.

Flight liberates the past. But only at intervals, without continuity. Flight is the present, bringing the past into the here and now. He remembers his period of 'success': fragments of triumph, then a sudden defeat which demanded a guilty person. So his success was not success; it prepared for his disgrace. Some people's guilt is decided. But that had been a long time ago. That had been the start of the recurrences. The important men decided who was guilty.

The important men were not important either. They were men short of breath who were able to live well but took no pleasure in it. He had been their creature; they financed him. He did not know them, he met them, they were abstractions. One does not know men who put up the finance; it's like making a bargain.

Were they then the kind of strong, challenging men, who plunge the world into war in order to keep the wheels turning? They were finicking men, primitively jocular with childish tastes. He did not remember them individually — only as men of a certain profession, a certain class — just as they must have seen him as a man of *his* profession, a technician ('Rather difficult to recall the name every time...').

One of the important men said, 'Doesn't it ever strike you how fortunate you are? It's as if you always get the green light.'

And it struck him for the first time. It had been in the period of the elongated cars. They slithered in aristocratic elegance among the more popular vehicles, dashes in the Morse code of the traffic. His elongated caress of a vehicle seldom encountered a red light, it was true.

'Good fortune isn't everything.'

'A great deal, all the same. Not an element — a catalyst.'

People talked to him in the language of technology, to make themselves understood.

'A catalyst is a phenomenon that can be calculated.'

'Those who are fortunate calculate their good fortune. As long as it lasts.'

'And when it doesn't last?'

'Then they still calculate for it, unfortunately.'

Conversations over the dinner table after a conference, a table from which the important men served themselves small helpings, for the sake of their health. After all, the world depended on them. And imagined conversations between an 'I' and a 'me'. Conversations about small matters, concealed warnings — such as this one about good fortune; petty gibes that were meant to be thought over at leisure.

Somebody remarked, 'It's the same where ambition is concerned.'

'But I'm not ambitious.'

'As with ambition. Nobody is ambitious. It's simply there — others' ambition. Including one's own — which one does not have.'

'Is that how it is with good fortune?'

'Precisely. Others' good fortune. So one seeks it out. There are people who *pray* — quite ungodly persons. They have no faith, but they pray, they pray for good fortune. They tell the secret god they do not believe in: You help others, after all. Send your rain on the unjust fellow as well as on the just. Here I am.'

'Everyone is a swindler, you mean?'

'Everyone is enormously self-deluded. If self-delusion was as illegal as swindling, everyone would be given life imprisonment.'

'Perhaps they have been?'

'You said something there, young man!'

Unimportant conversations about unimportant matters. That was the past, the past he remembers. What were the important matters? The important thing is that solemn men sit together beneath the cannon smoke of their cigars, placing words in the scale. The scale is invisible, like words, but it is there. Finally it tips, it tips the way it is supposed to go, towards the side of the important man, the one who is most important. He says nothing when all the others have spoken. Then the scale tips.

Important men do not speak until afterwards. The most important of them said, 'Military preparedness isn't solely a question of armaments and defence, but a matter of all countries producing things that are unprofitable in order to be "self-sufficient", in case. And "in case" means war. In Australia they plant fir trees with state support in order to produce timber for various purposes. Scandinavia could provide them with better timber. In one small country called Norway they cultivate grain, even though the best they can hope for is that it will ripen at all, once a year only. In other places grain is harvested three times a year; their production is enormous. Why do they do it? In order to be self-supporting — in case. Nearly everything is a form of preparedness. Eight pence out of every ten allotted goes to preparedness in one form or another, to subsidizing what is entirely unreasonable. It's called self-help, a so-called peaceful pursuit, but it makes everyone a little more capable of waging war — in case. What then? I expect *your* conscience troubles you because you contribute to war in your minuscule way? Everyone contributes to war, always. Does it disturb you?'

'The idea of war disturbs me.'

'The idea of death disturbs everyone. That doesn't prevent us from dying.'

'The idea that we organize death for — everyone.'

'So that disturbs you! Well, well. Does impregnation disturb you — it doesn't? Perhaps what disturbs sensitive people is that they're alive at all. No, no, I admit it's a responsibility. It's just that it's not so easy to see how to free oneself from it. Oh — some make an end of it. I can't understand the logic of it; it's no way for a conscience to go, at the most a way out. Well — I can offer you one consolation:

conscience is a disease that affects you less seriously the second time it attacks. Afterwards one becomes immune.'
'Or the opposite!'
'Well, that's your opinion. Like most diseases it causes trouble to others. But you're probably right. One should never do anything one regrets in advance. Did you get fifty thousand for your services? A mistake, it has already been rectified. It should have been a hundred thousand.'
'We were talking about conscience.'
'Two hundred thousand, as I said. The mistake has been rectified.'

Another of the important men: 'Our young friend thinks in a kind of poetic subjunctive. But that should not be confused with imagination. The imagination is an extension of the possible. — Everything *can* become possible? Correct. Gradually, as the imagination extends our perspective. But imagination is conservative.'
Protests: 'The imagination is conservative?'
'The imagination is cautious. Think how long it has taken to arrive at any technical progress. The imagination is biological.'
'The imagination is absolutely unlimited!'
'Precisely. Biological — that is to say in our case humanly lawful, therefore bound by what is limitless.'
'That's what we said!'
'What was said, yes. Bound by the humanly limitless, what we regard as limitless.'
Protests, weaker: 'There are no limits!'
'No?'

He grasps his head in his hands. He is standing where the path divides, holding his head in his hands. Are these memories or merely humming words?
And the answer, from railway stations and crossroads, where the path of the fugitive divides over and over again, is that one does not remember the place of each decision; everything merely exists — to begin with, then it disappears. The impurities are left: what suits the organism, what it can come to terms with for the sake of its 'conscience'.

He is reminded of the names of businesses, powerful during his period of 'success' in the country where he had been living then: Merlin & Gerlin, Labinal, Sté La Précision Mécanique, Kuhlmann, Emile Soutage... each powerful name a concept, an ogre, every important man a smooth or fastidious man, slightly democratic according to the demands of the time, without greatness.

From an after-dinner conversation: 'What *is* greatness?'
'Oh no, young man, you mustn't ask questions like that. Coffee is served. Not that I can drink it.'
'Everyone was an infant once, a demanding infant...'
Raised eyebrows.
'Innocent!'
Glances sideways. 'That young man didn't have more than one brandy, did he?'

Dialogue at a pavement café. The important man is speaking again.
'A city bombed during the last war, or the next, what of it? It will turn into a modern city overnight, an undreamt of city, without slums, a city envied by the neighbouring town, which was spared and simply remains as it was.'
'We ought not to forget that there were people who — '
'Excuse me, I didn't hear...'
'I said, don't forget the people — '
'It must be the noise from the street!'
'Forget the people!'
'Well now, there we *are* in agreement. We have to forget about the people.'

Solitary thoughts after spending time with important men whom one does not know:
My brain can handle certain predetermined matters which will be demanded of me, ceaselessly and in many countries. I'm a technician. Who's going to cry for me? I'm not even one of those men who shoot game first, and shed tears over a dead animal afterwards.
The voice: 'Isn't that exactly what you are?'

'I've made my choice, I tell you!'
'Or left it to others to choose. Left it to fate to decide?'
'It has cost me something: deliberation.'
'Call it conscience; be reckless, call it something superior. Say your heart bleeds on behalf of humanity. Be modest and reckless at the same time. Call your earnings good fortune and indulge in a little remorse. It whets the appetite.'
'I'm a technician, as I said. I know nothing about the plans of the important backers.'
'They have none. You know that very well. They have backers as well.'
'*They're* accountable!'
'Everyone is an exception. That's part of the rules of the game.'
'Which game?'
'Ha ha ha ha!'

An echo during sleepless nights: 'Ha ha ha ha...'
'At any rate, I'm the person who'll be sacrificed if there's any blunder.'
Muttered responses from the four corners of the earth: 'Listen to him now. Already starting to accept his guilt, that delicious guilt, balm of hurt souls.'

After his disgrace, his reply to the experts during the investigation: 'I'm not complaining. I may have been merely the pitcher which was sent to collect water so often that it came back without its handles. I relied on the accountability of others, of those who take their authority for granted; more than that, who take themselves for granted. Since they are unique they are unable to observe themselves. They're blind, and I wanted to be like them. My nature is to take nothing for granted in a person. I've always been a doubter — about everything. But action was demanded. Lack of accountability is contagious.'
The experts' report:
'An exponent of the milieu. Maximum IQ. Weak ethical judgement. Periods of self-pity. Uses expressions like 'the amorality of energy'. Lacks the ability to see himself in relation to his actions,

and therefore to see things in perspective. Expresses surprise that it should be taken for granted that there is any connection between events merely because they concern one and the same person. Is completely sceptical concerning a lasting, let alone unchanging, identity. Considers his periods of passivity as the happiest and most valuable morally. Expects periods of renewed activity and automatically reduced faculty of judgement. Employs terms such as 'ill-fated activities'. Compares them to thunderbolts.'

And while he sat stitching industrial gloves in the hall of the big house, ideas about time and action, expressed in monologues, mouth closed so as to escape notice:

It's possible to decide on the course of time oneself, whether it is to be long or short. It's possible, for instance, to cause a very long period of time to disappear by absolutely never exposing oneself to any kind of crisis.

It's possible to make time pass rapidly; with a little practice one can banish it altogether as well. It's a matter of turning oneself into nothing, then time vanishes too. When one's independent of the weather, one can create good weather for the mind almost continuously. It's a question of practice, of keeping the thunderbolts out of one's life. One can cease to be irritated or to make objections; one can accept everything. I've just read in a newspaper that a separatist group in a disturbed country organized an armed revolt and occupied the broadcasting company, the airports and the public buildings. As a result they were masters of the country for twenty four hours. The participants were executed for the sake of making an example. There is already talk of 'the ones who were really guilty'.

Isn't that how we think of God? Sitting omnisciently, with a resigned smile, achieving nothing by means of the pathetic mechanism he set in motion in the dawn of time? Those who are caught are guilty. What is meant by 'really guilty'? That kind of newspaper acts in its own brief way on behalf of humanity as it were, perpetually hunting for someone who is even more guilty, most guilty; as if there were an indestructible being behind it all at whom they were shaking their fists. Oh, all those imaginary thieves who are allowed to escape, while the trees rattle towards nightfall with the small corpses of thieves with impaired mental capacities... Important people had better watch out. Their hour will certainly come!

But their hour does not come. For important people change places. Besides, they are so very, very unimportant. Exponents of the environment. Exponents of public opinion which they themselves have created. In short, exponents. The newspaper shakes its fist heroically at an imagined initiator, Evil incarnate, someone who inaugurates disaster and the guilty conscience in turn and in uninterrupted sequence: a rationalistic Satan.

Thus God sits in his prison, knowing it all. It's good to be God and to stitch gloves and shoes. God created the serpent, not in his own image, but he created it. Now the serpent has struck with its tail, so they chop some of it off. But the serpent survives. They don't chop off its head; it hasn't struck with its head yet. When *that* strikes it will be quite another matter. Then it will be justified retaliation, or the best defence, or simply for God's own sake and above all in his name, tum-ti-tum-tum! But no! For the time being it has only struck with its tail, and the tail is not entitled to strike. An example must be made of it; heads must roll for the sake of the tail. God knows this, he who sits stitching gloves among other exponents. Some of them have had an unhappy childhood and some of them a happy one, but the one is just as bad as the other. They are all exponents and doomed to deep reflection, justice enfolds them with all the untiring consideration which is its duty, and thus the world gets better and better until the moment when the head is found at which everyone is shaking his fist. They used to call it the Devil, but that's a bit old-fashioned and lacking in psychology. The Devil was driven out — pure foolishness. Now we shake our fists.

The large institution, which lies outside the smaller institution in which he sits stitching gloves, is called Freedom. There they train half-experienced psychologists and wholly experienced lunatics. The psychologists are gods too, or almost like God: *they* know everything or almost everything. Not that they do anything about it either. All they can do is to separate the exponents from the sheep; that's what they know about. Their file concerning unhappy childhoods is more extensive than the file in the neighbouring country, which is underdeveloped: there they hang thieves head downwards. They must be hanged head up; that's progress. The 'really guilty' are still on the waiting list, but it's a sign of great progress to know they're there.

The same newspaper says that a certain shot in a street is supposed to have provoked the smaller revolution, which might have started a greater one, had there been no interference. It was even more unfortunate that three or four of the important people were supposed to be meeting at that precise moment in order to prepare for a meeting between the most important men in the world. There is, moreover, a picture of them, looking small and pained: one has a paunch, another a little fart of a moustache, a third, wearing spectacles and a long mane of hair, is supposed to have smiled on arrival.

And he thinks, resigned and untroubled as far as he himself is concerned, are they in good faith — in that faith that is so good that they are invulnerable; or is their professional innocence authorized for the good of the whole, like the good faith of a judge or of an expert adviser? The atmosphere in the long corridors, in the antechamber, the brave face full of confidence in shady dealings — does that automatically free them from accountability? Are the important people — confined in a cage of deference — so liberated from their own selves that they are capable of saying in good faith: It was not I... ?

Perhaps they can say, I became what people assumed I was — and then bow obliquely to the last judge and enter into the joy of their Lord. The sacred average has exonerated them in advance. It is called the majority, and has come about because somebody divided the total by a number. The result is an exponent — again an exponent; it is called the People and is infallible. It is the People's right to find the guilty, small persons guilty of small things, and to dream of great guilty persons for the total. On the other hand, someone who has been branded as guilty has the advantage of being able to reason objectively about these matters: to be God and objective, without motive or remorse, as long as he is guilty. The court is in all cases on the side of the majority: the calculated average. And the spokesman of the average: the newspaper in his hand, authorized to understand nothing on behalf of the majority.

All this surfaces because I am a fugitive again. Those who flee remember the past in fragments, they remember it piecemeal, it becomes like a splintered pane of glass. Was such a pane ever whole? Impossible to tell, for at the time when it might have been whole it was not then the past, and it was impossible to have any perspective on it.

There was more freedom in being a prisoner in the big house. There was an anonymous fellowship about it which relieved the gnawing ego; there one was free of this freedom which leads to disaster because it incites to action.

Later came recuperation at a hotel in the country. One was a person with a past, a besmirched past. How does the past look in unbesmirched condition? Can it be seen at all?

Now he knows: the stains *are* the past. Are stains produced when small and slightly larger important men have crossed one's own minuscule path on their powerful journeys? They must be.

'After all, you could have chosen something else — had a chicken farm. There's always something for a clever brain to do.'

'I suppose the fact is that one finds an interest, develops ability, acquires an education.'

Echoes from ironic know-alls:

'Ambition, as we said.'

Echoes from those wise after the event and keeping to the safe side: 'What did we tell you? Certain persons get on better inside the walls. As soon as you've rid yourself of us you'll find playmates with whom to cultivate your inclinations.'

Words of wisdom from all the wise men, one after the other:
'What did I tell you?'
'What did I tell you?'
'What did I tell you?'

The whole truth surfaced — too late in the second of the thunderbolt — at the moment when someone inside the bar said, '*He's coming.*'

11

Matias Roos peered into a murky room. Dark beams and half-timbered walls along with thick pillars of sombre wood, faded away inwards. It must have been the remaining part of what was originally a house, an enormous bar which dissolved into corners and enclosures, where solid oak tables were revealed in the cone of light from the huge chandelier which threw a diffuse glow over the nearest of them. Diagonally across to the left he saw a low door which presumably led to the street, or perhaps a narrow alley. No light came through the window pane in the door; no noise. On the wall beside the door hung an old-fashioned barometer. That part of the bar had the appearance of a ship.

The heavy door fell to behind him. He took a pace forward. A man with a white apron advanced from the imposing counter to the right. His slack mouth moved soundlessly; it must have been his voice that had said, 'He's coming'. The man looked at him fixedly with tiny eyes almost hidden by yellow folds of fat. Otherwise he was as white as the apron he was wearing round his heavy stomach. There was something officious about him, half servile, half insolent; it lay in his expectant posture and it increased the uncertainty Matias Roos had felt from the instant he entered. Then he caught sight of the other people in the bar, and as he glanced from person to person — not so much the faces, for only the fat bartender was looking at him — he was given the impression of something familiar, something from long ago, like the features of persons in a dream one is already forgetting.

The feeling filled him with distaste. His instinct was to turn back to gain time, to return to the cold staircase, away from everything soft and carpeted and uncertain, back to the chilly visibility which, from the outset, had roused his memories of what had brought him there.

Then the bartender stepped forward and said, 'Good evening'. He said it courteously and impersonally. Matias Roos lost his resolve to turn back and took another step forward into the room. But the bartender left him at once and approached a young couple who were sitting further away in the gloom. 'May I take...' he said, professionally courteous. But the young couple turned their backs on him. '... your order?' continued the bartender pointlessly into thin air. There was something apathetic about his behaviour. Next he turned towards a well-dressed man in his sixties, who was sitting even further away, also with his back to him. 'May I take — ?' But it seemed as if his courtesy towards the well-dressed elderly man was dissimulated, even demonstrative. He was given no answer either, the well-dressed man merely giving a slight shrug of the shoulders.

The bartender, checked in his officious round, also shrugged his shoulders and sighed, 'Very well.' Then he went across to the window on the same side as the door and the barometer and said, half to himself, as he looked out, 'Same miserable weather.'

Matias Roos tried to see through the thick coloured panes. The weather had not been miserable when he was standing out in the street. But was it the same day? Suddenly days did not matter any more.

'Ladies and gentlemen,' said the bartender, half turning away from the window. 'It's still raining.' Nobody reacted to his remark. He went to the barometer, tapped it, and said, 'It's at Change. Ladies and gentlemen, I permit myself to ask, What change?'

Matias Roos was about to answer him out of politeness. For a moment he felt sorry for this busy fellow who was trying so hard to get a conversation doing. But at that moment the fat bartender went further into the room. A thin man was sitting at a table with some cobbler's tools in front of him. At the bartender's last remark about the weather he had picked up a flute. And now Matias Roos heard the same melancholy tune as he had heard outside, as he approached the door of the bar.

'Do stop it, Oliver!' roared the bartender all of a sudden. It was as if all the irritation he had not dared to vent on the other guests now flowed freely over the thin man with the flute and the cobbler's tools. But the thin man continued to play, if one could call it playing. There was no coherence in it, just a note here and there.

'Do you hear me, man?' But it was as if the energy had already gone out of the bartender's wrath. There was something resigned about his voice and the gesture which followed. 'No, he doesn't hear,' he said resignedly, and turned away from the thin flute player. The latter, however, stopped playing at once, at the very moment when the bartender gave up trying.

The bartender sniffed at the room. 'What's this?' He wrinkled his plump little nose. 'What quiet!' And he made these small remarks with an affected pathos, giving them a theatrical and empty ring, as if he had abandoned in advance all pretence of having any purpose in his questions. 'Do you hear, ladies and gentlemen?' he said in the same manner. 'It's completely quiet. Only the rain.'

And then Matias Roos heard that it was raining quietly and persistently outside. It was curious, he thought, with that sky, the light cirrus cloud above the dust. But then afterwards — hadn't it rained? He wondered vaguely about this question of the same day or time. He had met the uniformed men, but it might have been a long time ago. Again it occurred to him that he should disappear quietly, back to the cold corridors. There he could clarify his memories; there he could find his bearings towards some kind of action.

His decision was interrupted by a deep voice from the well-dressed man's table. 'Now listen, Mr Bartender, you're constantly making statements about things we can notice without your help.'

The man said it with his back to the room and it was impossible to guess whether he was irritated or had even noticed the bartender's restless activity. The bartender, on his part, jumped to attention, simulating pleasure at having achieved contact at last. 'What did the gentleman say?' he asked jovially. He sidled quickly towards the well-dressed gentleman's table. 'May I take ...?' But the impregnable back stopped him. 'So that's the way it is,' he said resignedly, approaching the table slowly nevertheless. Matias Roos watched the scene from where he was standing. There was something cantankerous about this fat bartender's friendliness, simultaneously aggressive and respectful. Now he leaned over the gentleman's shoulder and said, 'A game of dice perhaps? I'll wager, let's say a hundredth of what you owe me.'

Matias Roos felt apprehensive at this shameless impertinence. But the man at the table did not react. The bartender pointed at a huge black-board on the wall behind the counter. It held long columns of figures, written with chalk.

But the gentleman at the table did not turn to look at the blackboard. The bartender spoke again over his shoulder, rapidly, breathlessly. 'Shall I wager a tenth? A third? ... Or *everything*? We'll wipe out everything written on the blackboard, and its black surface will shine towards you again, blank and virginal. In other words you win, you are a free man, free, I said. Free of debt.'

Again it was as if he channelled all his energy into his superfluous verbosity with its theatrical turns of phrase. For when the man's back remained just as uninterested, the bartender straightened up and sighed a 'Very well, Mr Director, Sir'.

Matias Roos stood feeling active dislike for this fat fellow, less on account of his officious manner than because he allowed himself to be rejected so humiliatingly by a guest who clearly owed him money. It occurred to him that rich people like that could find themselves in the most degrading situation without cringing. If it had been he, Matias Roos, who had owed money for his expenses over a long period, and to such a repulsive swine of a bartender, he would have knuckled under and fallen into the fellow's power. He decided on the spot not to allow himself to be tempted by any offer of credit.

Just then the well-dressed man who had been called the director said, 'I prefer to play against myself.'

He said it to himself, demonstratively to himself. But the bartender was back immediately with his servile compliance. 'Yes, of course, naturally.' And then, with a touch of irony, 'So as to win every time, to run no risk. Very sensible.'

The door opened behind them. The waiter whom he had met before, who called himself the Auxiliary, came in from the carpeted corridor. Matias Roos turned towards him and nodded. But the modest auxiliary looked straight past him and held the door open for a small man with glassy features and a white cape over his shoulders.

'This way, please,' said Daniel, propelling the newcomer ahead of him to a more distant corner of the bar. There he switched on a lamp, suddenly illuminating a high chair, equipped as a barber's chair. Daniel immediately began soaping this new customer for a shave, keeping an eye on the others in the room as he did so.

They on their part seemed to notice nothing. The bar seemed to be the venue for many activities. The thin fellow they called Oliver had actually taken out his cobbler's tools instead of his flute, which he had laid carefully aside. Now he was sitting hammering at an old-fashioned boot, while Daniel, the auxiliary, grasped his knife and shaved his customer so that the lather flew. Suddenly a busyness came over the scene, in sharp contrast to the apathetic mood of a short while ago. Matias Roos felt more at ease. Never mind that it was all happening in a bar. He reserved judgement and accepted events as they occurred.

Daniel was a proficient barber. He circled round his customer with little professional questions: 'Would you like a heated towel?' And when his customer did not reply: 'Certainly.' He placed the warm cloth carefully over his customer's countenance, so that only his white nose stuck out, cold and glassy. 'A little astringent?' Daniel smoothed some liquid into his customer's face. He continued at tremendous speed: 'Something to refresh the face a little? Of course!' With lightning rapidity he dipped both hands into some ointment which he massaged into the customer's skin. 'Nothing like a little toning for the face.'

The bartender had moved towards them, and was standing observing this activity with a satisfied expression. 'You're an expert, my dear Daniel, one can see that at once. In my time I always told people, 'Start doing something'. I used to say, 'The only thing of importance is ...'

But this Daniel, who must have been the bartender's subordinate, did not even deign to give him a glance. The bartender, on his part, sighed resignedly and shrugged his shoulders. At that moment the person they called Oliver dropped the large boot on the floor. The bartender gave a start of irritation, pressed both hands to his temples, and groaned.

Matias Roos took a step forward and asked, 'Did you say, *in my time?*'

But he noticed that his voice was slurred by anxiety and lack of use over a long period. The bartender did not hear him, either. Nobody heard him. At that moment the well-dressed gentleman turned to the bartender and made a small gesture with his hand. It appeared to be graciously inviting. The bartender instantly accepted the invitation, if invitation it was: he sat down at the table. He took a chair from the young couple and moved it over to the gentleman's table, even though there was one there already. Matias Roos said softly, 'Do you have to insult each other?' And when the bartender had taken the chair and seated himself — only then — did he half turn towards the young couple and say casually, 'Do I have the lady and gentleman's permission?'

The couple did not seem to notice that anybody had taken any chair. They sat gazing at each other with shining eyes. Each seemed to be filled with the most profound admiration for the other.

'Thank you,' remarked the bartender ironically. For a moment he regarded the two beautiful young persons with satisfaction.

'Why did you take a chair from there?' asked the director. And when the bartender did not reply, 'Then I have no need to ask. I see you're expecting another guest. I thought so.'

'Prospective new guests,' said the bartender curtly and loudly, 'are always seated at Mr Financier's table.'

Matias Roos cringed at this new and deliberate impudence. 'Financier', he thought. That's exactly the impression one gets of this somewhat too self-assured back. But the bartender continued, as if to see how far he could go: 'It lies in the nature of the matter. Mr Financier will have the first chance.'

'To do what?' asked the director indifferently.

The bartender shrugged his shoulders and took up a beaker with dice from the side table.

'No, I'm not going to play,' said the director in irritation.

'The chance to make a new acquaintance,' said the bartender. 'To orientate oneself, so to speak.' The other replied, curt and annoyed, 'I've asked you to avoid saying "so to speak" in my presence.'

'I beg your pardon,' said the bartender at once. 'Your forgiveness, so to speak.' The director gave him a weary look: 'So you're expecting a new guest — oh, do stop this childish secrecy of yours!'

But the bartender merely threw out a hand, irritating the other even further. It was obvious that this composed man was tense and interested now, in some way in the power of the bartender. 'All right, as you please. Tell me, is he, is he — well, speak, man!'

The bartender raised his hands. 'My lips are sealed with seven seals.' And he counted up to seven on his fingers with exasperating slowness. 'But at any rate it's a man this time too,' said the director. 'Always men. Do women never come here?'

The bartender made one of his affectedly pompous movements, and gestured behind and above himself in the direction of Matias Roos, who had been about to take another step forward in order to draw attention to his presence. Instead he watched the bartender's gesture. Above the door by which he had entered was a gallery almost the length of the room, ending in a staircase down to where the barometer was hanging. On this gallery was painted in ornate letters: PARADISE.

'Oh, her!' said the director, shrugging his shoulders. Oliver on the cobbler's stool began to play at that moment, the same melody Matias Roos had heard on the staircase. Now it seemed to him to have happened long ago, so long ago that it appeared to be impossible for his mind to find its way back to it. Yet again, it was one of those places which — had led him here. And he was seized by a feeling of hopelessness, a feeling of finality, a feeling that this was the objective of his long flight.

Over at the table the bartender said, 'Men are more rational to talk to, you know, about money.'

The director shrugged unwillingly. 'Money, always money.'

'Everyone has his own interest,' said the bartender briskly. 'In my time it was always, "Cobbler, stick to your last"... your last, Oliver!' he roared, seizing his head as Oliver continued with his melody. Over in the illuminated corner Daniel had finished the face massage but was carrying on with all his professional skill: 'How about freshening up the scalp a little? Very well. Perhaps a little shampoo first?' And without waiting for an answer he set to work on the silent customer's head. Matias Roos could see that the bartender was observing everything around him, but at the same time was all ears when the director continued, 'Besides, you were slicing up chops a short while ago.' And now Matias Roos remembered that he had heard a chopping sound when he was out in the corridor. So it had *not* been long ago. 'That's always a sign that people are coming,' added the director.

And the bartender, in expansive mood, replied, 'You're an acute observer, Mr Director, Sir. No use fooling you. No use at all. What was I about to say? It goes along with your profession, so to speak, it goes along with your profession'.

The director did not hide his irritation. 'Why do you always say everything twice?' But the bartender took no notice. 'Goes along with your profession — did I, twice? That goes along with the profession too. With the profession.'

'I heard you!' yelled the director, losing control. He seized the dice. 'No, you're not going to play. I won't play with you. I've told you, I'm going to play alone.'

'As you please, as you please. Perhaps you're waiting for — somebody?' And he leaned forward in a manner that clearly repelled the man with the dice. 'Whom should *I* be waiting for?'

But the bartender parried him at once. 'No, I don't know, as I said, I don't know, one never knows.'

'What does one never know?'

But the bartender said, just as amiably, 'No, not at all. Nothing. One knows nothing!'

And if it had really been his purpose to annoy, he got what he wanted. The director swept up the dice. 'What is this nonsense? One knows nothing?'

'So to speak, Mr Director, Sir. One goes about one's own affairs, as they say, about one's own affairs, and then — one fine day — one goes there no longer.'

He seemed to have succeeded finally in getting the self-assured man with the dice where he wanted him, for the latter half rose, holding his trembling hands in front of him. 'What a lot of balderdash!' he shouted. 'One goes about precisely *here*. I, the Director, Mr Financier as you permit yourself to call me, do you really think I don't know that you've picked me out as a kind of common denominator, yes, a symbol, here, here *in your place*? Do you think I don't realize that this daily treadmill has brought about a certain — a certain schematization of existence, 'so to speak" as you say — indeed, that this existence, to speak plainly, threatens to become incredibly simple, tending towards *the typical*.'

The bartender bowed and said under his breath, 'You are most understanding.'

'Nonsense! Do you hear what I say? Nonsense!'

The bartender's voice became slightly firmer.

'I hear very well that you're saying nonsense.'

But the director interrupted him. 'So, we're going about precisely here. That fellow Daniel, shaving someone over there, is obviously helping you with all sorts of odds and ends — what do I know about it? A person who shares your idiotic imperturbability, reduced to a technician at your pleasure! And he — this skinny puff of wind you call Oliver, your musical cobbler whom you tyrannize to play your tune — yes, ha ha — your tune, for some reason which is crushingly immaterial to me. Do you hear? Immaterial. So what do you mean by saying that one does not go about here? We go about precisely here, let me tell you.'

He sat down heavily. Matias Roos felt highly uncomfortable at finding himself a witness to a dispute between two people who must have hated each other for a long time. He retreated a pace into the shadow beneath the gallery. But the bartender did not appear to be in the least offended.

'Well, yes, up to a point. While on the other hand — '

'Then come out with it!' shouted the director. But his wrath seemed to be diminishing already. The bartender continued, almost meekly, 'All I mean is, one has a certain hope — all one's life — a certain hope.'

'Of what?'

'Well now, of — of getting out of it. Of change.'

The director looked at him in undisguised astonishment. 'Of getting out of life?'

'Oh, life — how can you talk so, well, blasphemously, isn't that the word? I only mean getting out of — um, achieving a result, Mr Director, Sir — if you know what I mean.'

The other grunted, 'Why shouldn't I know what you mean?'

But the bartender continued with his own train of thought. 'Precisely. You were the man who watched the result, watched one result after the other, so to speak. What was I about to say, the result, perhaps you missed that? You're just the sort of man who understands. You were so wise — excuse me, you *are* so wise.'

Matias Roos noticed that the director lowered his head. His voice was gruff and stubborn. 'Yes, I'm wise.'

And the bartender came back at once with his reply. 'Precisely. Exactly. Understood people, understood their aims, their petty aims, all those people who hope for — yes, a result, or that something will change radically, isn't that so? Something decisive perhaps, I don't know.'

He laughed modestly into thin air, as one who hasn't the ability to express deep thoughts. But that kind of laughter clearly embarrassed the director.

'What are you laughing at now? You always laugh in the most idiotic places.' But the bartender continued to laugh his modest laughter, as he said, 'As we said. For you see, Mr Director — I almost said Mr Financier — that's perhaps precisely what never happens — yes, I was referring to the change, the result. Maybe it depends on how things proceed. I'm referring to the result, or to the sum total perhaps. I mean, it's not given to everyone to stick to what he was searching for, I mean what he wanted out of something. That's why it's important to keep it going, keep it going, as I said, if you understand me...'

He sat playing with the director's dice, sifting them through his fingers, as if wanting to insinuate that the director sought his results in this ridiculous game.

'You're looking at the dice,' remarked the director after a pause. 'I know you consider everything to be a game, a perpetual game. But what do you really know about it? In fact the game is beginning to come to an end, even to approach a result, the result we're aiming for. That's one of the many things you don't understand. And another thing. You're more than welcome to call me Mr Financier. It is, at any rate, the least of your insolences.'

The two men sat opposite one another like prize fighters waiting for a welcome move. Yet there was a difference. Matias Roos noticed it with an astonishment that froze the situation into his brain. The two men were not really opponents; they were imitations of two opponents who have reached a decisive stage. And the stage they had reached was the imitation of a decisive stage. The other people in the bar were not taking much notice of the episode either; they looked as if they were used to it.

'Like a repeat performance!' he muttered as he stood beneath the gallery. Decisions passed through him in waves, then vanished. After all, he had come to this place in order to — to find out something. Who was it who had just spoken of change? He could not abandon it now, the recollection of the past... he wanted to turn towards the door he had come in by, but the will to do so died away. Instead he felt a kind of optimism.

All he had to do was to attract attention. These people would surely accept him, explain one or two things, perhaps show him to a seat. He looked at the back of the flute-playing Oliver's neck, a thin neck, made for bending, a humble neck, even. Perhaps he was a man who had found his way? Such a man could not be filled with the same arrogance as the bartender with his pig's eyes or the irascible director who had finally abandoned his cover. And not like the couple enjoying each other's company; they did not take their eyes off one another for an instant. And where Daniel, the auxiliary, was concerned, he had ignored him as soon as he entered, though he might not have seen him in the darkness. The best thing in every way would be to accept the situation, then perhaps he would find the way out of this place, even though it might take a long time. From here he could find a way, and not become like these people, waiting. He seized his head in order to try to remember what he had wished for once upon a time, what change.

But as he was about to approach the thin flute-player, Oliver laid the instrument aside and turned to face the gallery above Matias Roos' head. Someone was coming out of a door up there. Oliver must have heard something before he had, for he had looked up at the gallery at the same moment as he had stopped playing.

The bartender had also lifted his face to the gallery, and said, with surprising friendliness, 'Oliver, it's your turn.'

Oliver got to his feet noiselessly, went across to the stairs and up them. Matias Roos could not see the person up there, but the expressions of the others told him that it was a woman. The faces followed her progress back along the gallery. Things would have to remain as they were; he dared not go forward into the room now that he had lost his focal point in the humble flute-player. His face, too, had seemed familiar as he passed him, but from an immensely long time ago. A thin face, almost emaciated, but with shining blue eyes, unnaturally large, filled with excited passion when they were turned to the gallery.

Daniel's voice tore him out of his train of thought. 'If you'd lean forward a little...' And suddenly this barber began singing at the top of his voice, 'Soap and water, soap and water, and some cream, and some cream!'

It relaxed the tension. Matias Roos was longing for some irresponsible company. He also felt a strong desire for alcohol and confidential conversation. Later, he thought, he could come to the point, and they would tell him about the frontier.

The word seemed more distant than ever. All his efforts, this burden of fragments from a past... The word frontier had stood out strongly and clearly once. He could have asked Oliver about that. He did not seem cheerful, this cobbler; nevertheless he seemed to have achieved something.

Perhaps, in spite of everything, Daniel — this jack of all trades with worldly experience... Later he could talk to the beautiful couple; surely they couldn't admire one another for ever? And as for the director — Good Lord, once he had known people like that in the life outside: him or one like him. They had been called Important Persons...

In life...! He remained standing as if stuck fast in his situation. 'People like that' was how he had judged those men, the men of power who had betrayed him. So perhaps he ought to hate this man, not just observe him? Peter Gustov had said that we always meet again.

He took a step forward. The rotting wooden floor swallowed up the sound. He coughed. It struck him as an instant of incredible daring. The bartender rose from the director's table. The director said, 'He's coming!'

The bartender stood with his back to Matias Roos. 'You have very sharp ears, Mr Director,' he said.

'I have very sharp *hearing*. Do be kind enough to express yourself precisely. I have very sharp hearing, very sharp sight and a very sharp intellect.'

Bartender: 'And yet you were mistaken.'

Matias Roos dared not move.

Director: 'Mistaken! What do you mean?'

'The person you're waiting for is not coming.'

'I'm not waiting for anyone.'

The bartender threw out his fat hands. 'Then we'll agree on that, we'll agree on that.'

An irritated grimace passed over the director's face. 'And besides, it's a matter of complete indifference to me who comes or does not come to this place.'

The bartender, sitting down: 'We'll agree on that, as I said.'
Daniel placed a bell-shaped object over the head of his customer. He lit a cigarette and walked straight towards Matias Roos in the half-dark.

It was now or never. A situation like this could not last for ever. He heard the bartender say, '*You're* waiting for a person for whom you've made it possible — '

And the director: 'I demand — hm, well, I ask you to keep all previous relationships out of our existence here.'

And the bartender again: 'Yes, of course. Of course. Now that our existence has *stabilized* itself.'

And he said this with a vicious intonation that roused a protest in Matias Roos. What kind of existence did this potbelly consider to be tenable?

He took a couple of steps forward towards Daniel. He heard the bartender say, 'Hush! I can hear your — what was I about to say? Our friend, our pride...'

Matias Roos felt his heart hammering. This was the situation he had expected, which he had perhaps himself caused — that *he* was the person they were waiting for.

Daniel came straight towards him and said, in a completely normal voice, 'Good evening.'

Matias Roos could not utter a word. His throat was constricted. Now he saw himself in the picture. But he could not decide on his actions. It was as if being brought into the picture made him part of the mechanism: he was instantly controlled by the functioning of the picture itself. From this moment on the picture decided for him. As if he were an old customer he walked towards the counter and behind it. With his left hand he took a bottle from the shelf; with his right he picked up the chalk which was lying there, noted the label on the bottle and wrote on the board in a steady hand. He had done this always, it was as if the whole of his period of waiting had been due to the oversight of a daily task. He took a glass, went forward in front of the counter and across towards the table where the director was sitting. The bartender stood in his way.

'That seat is taken.'

Matias Roos saw the raised faces of the young couple. For a moment they had ceased to admire one another. Their faces expressed a certain pre-occupied tension. He thought — or he acted as if he was thinking: it's important to ignore this bartender; I'm in the picture, I'm a *part* of it. He nodded briefly at the director and placed the bottle and the glass on the table. At once Daniel was beside the table, offering him a cigarette. Something inside him thought, this is going well. He took the cigarette without thanking him, and was given a light. Then he poured the drink into the glass.

The director looked at him: 'Well?'

'What do you mean by that?' Matias Roos lifted the glass to his lips.

The director, imperturbable: 'I mean, what extraordinary discovery have you made today? What would you like me to interest myself in?'

Matias Roos emptied the glass. The director turned to the bartender.

'You see what a high price he puts on himself! The same play-acting every time!'

They looked at each other like a couple of conspirators — the very people who had hated each other an instant ago. Was he not part of the picture after all?

Bartender: 'You're right. The same play-acting, exactly the same play-acting.'

The bartender sat playing with the dice. Now he looked straight at Matias Roos.

'Would you like a turn at the dice? — No? As you please.' He got to his feet and spat out, 'You can be as ingenious as you like, but you've never invented dice that will always win for you.'

'Who has?' asked Matias Roos against his will.

And the bartender, curtly: 'Who? Oneself. And now you'll say "Oneself?" — the opponent is also oneself! That's what you'll say. I know you.'

Matias Roos felt a familiar hopelessness rise in him. He replied, again against his will, with a well-known phrase: 'The opponent always wins.'

And the bartender, curt again, with cunning little eyes: 'QED. So much talent! So much — talent.'

He got to his feet, fat, but remarkably agile. There was a concentrated power about this bartender as he walked over to Daniel, who had seated himself together with the young couple. He said, as he walked, 'I'm not saying a word, not a word, as I said. Not a word.' He remained standing, drumming with his fingers on the back of Daniel's chair.

'Not a word.'

Matias Roos felt himself under great pressure. He had made himself known at this place, openly and honestly. He had accepted its customs, and then been greeted with insolence.

But it was not too late to turn back — at least, not too late to turn his back on this fat bartender with his pig's eyes. Now he noticed: he had seen eyes like that before, in short-sighted persons who normally wear glasses and then suddenly take them off: a perplexed expression on an exposed face.

Matias Roos turned abruptly to the director and said earnestly, again to his own astonishment:

'Have you noticed, Mr Director, that when you come out on to your doorstep in the morning, about to put on your gloves, that you always take the wrong glove first?'

The director's face looked tired and troubled. Matias Roos was beside himself at this lack of interest. He rose to his feet, gesturing; it became extremely important to him that this self-satisfied man should understand what he meant.

'What I mean is, since you mentioned inventions, one tries — for one reason or another, which incidentally I believe I know, but that's beside the point — one tries to put the right hand glove on the left hand, and that's — annoying...'

The director looked up. There was no doubting his disdain.

'Is this the result of your lengthy deliberation?'

'It's annoying, as I said. I'm not thinking so much of the time wasted, no, but of the distraction of the moment, this concentration on something of no importance for the tenth of a second. It can be — momentous.'

He poured himself another drink and raised the glass to his mouth quickly, as if to dispel the embarrassing impression of drivel. The director said, with a politeness which was even more embarrassing than his previous coldness, 'I'm not sure that I understand what you mean.'

'But think again! At the moment when a person goes out of his door and life is about to open out before him, at that moment this person is already on his way, on his way, let me tell you, from a more or less static condition in an enclosed space *towards* an existence which calls on his efforts. He is, in other words, open to all possibilities, to that constellation of impulses, of results of some previous occurrence, of decision-creating impressions — in short, open to that life which lays claim to all his abilities in these precious seconds when the mind is open.'

He shouted this. He knew that he was overwhelmed by his unfortunate urge to embroider, to digress; it came of a long period of loneliness. But he was already possessed by the urge to see the raised heads, the listening faces.

'And what happens?' he continued dramatically. 'This person steps out of his door, the door is fashioned so that it slams and locks itself automatically behind him, not so quickly that it surprises him, but not so slowly either that he needs to think about closing it. The steps he is walking down are suitably shallow, so that no unexpected impressions will be communicated to his body. Space opens itself to him! Outside the street is paved, just so that his mind shall not be detained by anything unimportant in these seconds when something which can be of service to mankind begins to occupy his brain: a business transaction, a gigantic design, a painful detail in a chain of reasoning, something which releases this chain — so long as he is not distracted...'

He paused. He noticed that it was precisely the wealth of detail that had begun to influence his listeners.

'Without thinking he reaches into his inside pocket for his gloves. He takes both gloves in one hand, and — voilà! The thumb is on the wrong side!'

Matias Roos wiped his forehead; he felt tension rising in him. The bartender said, 'The thumb is on the wrong side?'

He held both his hands up in front of him like small dishes. He laughed, and sent Matias Roos a doubtful glance. The director coughed.

I'm winning a small victory now, thought Matias Roos.

'What happens? The man loses all his concentration, all his precious dreams, the creative atmosphere of his hallowed goal. And this can never be won back. The unfinished mood cannot continue after an interruption. It is not like repairing a railway line.'

The bartender showed his amusement again. 'A railway line!' he shouted in delight.

But the director sent the bartender a withering glance. 'Proceed!'

'My little idea naturally attempts to remove this difficulty with the help of a glove which fits both hands equally well — a mere detail of cut.'

The director, fatigued: 'And you consider this to be important?'

Matias Roos knew he must fight.

'It is, at least, a matter of small dimensions, a trifle which cannot cause accidents, something with a certain intimacy...'

'There's something insane about this admiration of trifles. You are, to put it briefly, afraid. Pull yourself together, man, start on something serious again.'

And, once more, that 'again', seemed so close, so familiar, as if they had talked about everything before.

'You mean something real?'

He felt his anxiety rising in him, anxiety at approaching what they called real.

'I mean something of importance. You know very well what I mean.'

Matias Roos sat down heavily. An inexplicable certainty of having 'come to the point' came over him.

'As *you* know better than anyone else, I have done things that were called serious. Did it turn out for the good of mankind? No, no!' he shouted in sudden irritation. His critical consciousness acquired a life of its own beneath this mask of assertion. Why was he sitting here, assuming that this man was a phantom from those days, a *representative* of...? And besides, he could see already from the man's ironic smile that he was expecting gross banalities. The exhaustion against which he had fought so long — indeed, for as long as he could remember — returned, that too like an echo of the situation.

'I'll spare you banalities. Everything was for the best for human beings, for mankind if you like. If I've turned to the small things in life since then — but you're not listening to me.'

'Because I know what's coming. I supported you once. *We* gave you a chance. You were a small man in a small laboratory. You were interested in both the biggest and the smallest matters, such as manufacturing a coffee substitute that caused heart complaints, because people demand the bad along with the good. You see these dice? They have six sides, six possibilities, only one of them is *the* possibility. You were a dice with twelve possibilities, perhaps more. Who is going to take any interest in the ten or eleven which are unimportant?'

Matias Roos felt the stream of things familiar and unfamiliar pass through him; uncontrollable reminiscences, displaced memories from an existence forgotten until this moment. And he noticed — during this flow of dreamed or experienced events from the past — that everything surrounding him at this moment was the same in another way, perhaps even in the same way, only impaired, as if behind blue-tinted glass, some distance further from the reality in which he had tossed about blindly: active and blind, conscious and blind, calculating and blind. He supported his head on his hand. 'Yes, yes, yes, yes...'

But the other interrupted in conciliatory fashion. 'The person who gives a weak man a chance gets no thanks for it. You must forgive me for repeating it: that part of your thought process which does not concern technical matters still does not interest me. As a friend of man you are as hollow as ever.'

He wanted to ask, 'as when?', but his energy failed him. There was this Daniel as well, this auxiliary. His bottles and perfumes were filling the bar with a sickly smell. He started up a vibrator. The director was forced to raise his voice.

'And in addition, when you began on this *other*, as you call it, this faculty which humans lack — wasn't that intimacy? No, no, I expect you're right. Why don't you go out into the wilderness? Give the birds of the air the chance to share your wisdom. Or shut yourself in. It cannot possibly have to do with a pair of gloves.'

Matias Roos bored his fingers into his throbbing temples. He said, 'You and your dice. Why don't you make a die with sixes on every side? When all this goes on and on — there must surely be some purpose in minimizing the guilt, in finding the smallest starting point. Don't you understand?'

The director looked at him squarely. 'No. Nor do you.'

He leaned forward. There was actually friendliness in his face which had only performed official social functions. 'You're on the wrong track. You'll always be on the wrong track with this unfortunate tendency to try to make sense of petty matters. What do you call it? To find meaning. — Someone's coming.'

Bartender: 'My compliments, Mr Director. You have very sharp ears.'

He went to the little door which seemed to lead out into the street.

The director watched his movements cautiously. How was it possible that this fat fellow with the small eyes could hypnotize such a man?

'You're not listening to me?'

The director: 'No!'

The bartender threw out his arms in a theatrical gesture. 'Greetings, arm of the law! May I shake the hand of the law?'

The person who entered slung a black rain cape to one side, and with it the outstretched hand. He resembled a bird: dark wings, pointed nose.

Matias Roos acted from old instinct. He withdrew without hesitation to the furthest end of the long counter where it was almost dark.

The man shook the water from his cape and walked quickly into the bar room. His gait, too, was as rapid and staccato as a bird.

'Mr Director... Daniel — you're a barber today?' He turned to the beautiful couple, to the customer.

'Is nobody else here?'

The man picked up the empty glass left by Matias Roos and sniffed at it.

The bartender made a resigned gesture towards the gallery. Then he took the glass out of the man's hand. 'May I offer you something?'

The man turned abruptly. He looked like an imitation of a detective. He took up his position in front of the young couple.

'And you?'

The young lady regarded him with a lingering gaze.

'We are the main characters,' she said.

'Which main characters?'

The beautiful young man looked at him, his expression childish. 'The main characters. The ones who get each other at the end.'

His partner interrupted him. 'That is, unless one of us dies. Then it will be a tragedy.'

'Precisely,' said the young man. 'If she dies.'

'I?' she cried out. 'Where on earth do you get that idea?'

The young man lifted his eyes to heaven and invited them all to be his witnesses. 'Are you starting on that again? Surely you didn't seriously think that I would be the one who died?'

'For heaven's sake!' The young woman turned to the detective. 'Have you ever heard such a thing in all your life? *I'm* supposed to die — !'

'Don't listen to her!' The young man turned to face her. '*If*, that's all I mean — only *if*.'

'And then you'd simulate Sorrow — you who don't own...'

'Watch what you say now — you who can't even ...'

But she interrupted him, sweet as honey. 'Tell me, my darling, what is it I can't do?'

He did not look at her, but focused his gaze out into space, delighted.

'Nothing, my love. You resemble the moon, which borrows its light from — '

He caressed his body with both hands.

The bartender turned to the new arrival. 'Charming young people. I have faith in the young; there's something so candid about them.'

The young lady rose in a fury and left the room. Matias Roos felt the cold draught of air as she walked past him and out through a small opening at the end of the counter; he had not noticed it before. He shrank back so as not to be seen.

The man in the cape said, 'Oh, so there's another door! I see that if you want to learn anything here you must find it out for yourself.'

'After all, you *are* the detective,' said the bartender with satisfaction.

But the director interrupted him.

'Why are you preventing the authorities from carrying out their work?'

The bartender, curtly: 'I must say, *you* didn't help the authorities very much in your time either.'

And that *in your time* went once more like a chill through Matias Roos, that unpleasant chill on experiencing an echo.

The bartender rounded it off sarcastically: 'Besides, things must take their course as far as I'm concerned, their protracted course.'

A fire alarm sounded far away. Everyone got to his feet and listened. They heard fire engines approaching; the din increased into a cacophony so penetrating that objects trembled: sirens, steam whistles, bells. Words came into Matias Roos' mind: 'as if it were the end of the world...' Then the noise died away. Matias Roos stood in the innermost recess of the corner and saw that the bartender and the director were looking at him.

'Accusingly,' it said inside him, 'as if I were the guilty one.' And the word *guilty* remained hanging in the air, like the sound of a bell.

The detective had walked across to the opaque windows beside the barometer. The bartender said, 'Fire again, fire and destruction everywhere. I don't understand it.'

The detective turned on his heel abruptly. 'You don't?'

The director, apologetically: 'So much happens, *we* can't help it.'

The detective turned towards him in the same manner. 'You can't?'

The director flinched. Then he took courage.

'What's the real reason for coming here — prying? You must forgive me, but we're simply *here*. I wasn't the final authority. Who are you really?'

'It's my duty to — pry, as you put it, to investigate the state of affairs, how things are, to investigate the *guilt*. You can call me the detective; I know you do behind my back. It's not easy for me either, let me tell you, when everyone tries to hide his guilt. Around here they call me the Almighty.'

He made a vague and inclusive gesture with his arm beneath the rain cape.

12

The moment of the Thunderbolt had not passed. Oliver came down from the gallery and began to play softly. The young woman again slid into her seat beside her beautiful friend. The director scattered the dice indifferently on to the table.

Matias Roos looked at them all. In a moment he would recognize them. Things had been coming to a head since he stepped into this room. Now the bartender approached him, snatching the flute from Oliver as he passed. The ingratiating smile had been wiped off his face and an unhappy expression drifted across the fat features. The bartender, said, this time without the affectation that had made him so odious, 'You know me, don't you?'

'Peter Gustov! Maybe I did know — that it was you.'

'No embraces! We're all on formal terms here. Do I understand that you wished to communicate something about your childhood?'

Matias Roos looked about him. How had anyone guessed at thoughts that had touched on that lost paradise for less than a second? But he knew his surprise was simulated. Everything was as it had to be.

'Wenche!'

But the beautiful young woman wrapped her smile in cellophane.

The young man, Bernhard, said, 'Let's not name names. Haven't you been allotted your role?'

Daniel, the auxiliary, came forward slowly. Matias Roos stared into his vulgar, attractive face, trying to place it. Daniel smiled cheekily back.

'You *did* mention a name in the corridor upstairs, but let's forget it. You're trying to tell us something all the time. The bartender is right. Just tell us the story. *That's* your role — don't you understand?'

Matias Roos knew what was coming, but he dissimulated, weakly looking for an excuse. 'What story?'

Daniel: 'Stop playing about. The story of your childhood, of course. The story of the English chair.'

Matias Roos looked about him, wanting to sit down. The bartender was beside him at once with a chair, pushing him down on it. The room slowly dissolved. The voice he heard was his own.

13

From the ashes of memory there leaps a single, protracted spark, like a chemical analysis of pain. Acids and liquids of all colours and differing densities whirl, crystals are formed without any sense of direction. It is painful, painful. Suddenly it ceases. The colours are collected into a dominant, the red is produced by the common will. All that is whirling loses importance. One thing remains, standing immovable in the memory, the English chair.

It stood in a loft, a rickety loft in a rickety outhouse with a woodshed beneath it, where the smell of sawdust and damp wood was overpowering. The floor was a soft carpet of wood shavings.

But from this cushion a flimsy ladder led up to the loft above. Up there the walls had shrunk, the light penetrated in shafts, a parade of shafts that pierced the eye. It was an exciting climb, for the ladder gave beneath the climber, and the floor at the top gave beneath those who crept on it. No question of walking upright. And in spite of the shafts of light it was murky up there too. Dust covered the shrunken floor, but the air was fresh, as if it were a sky above the musty shed below. In the corners lay a mattress, the frame of a table, and various implements which had seen better days.

But furthest in, where it was darkest, illuminated only by one or two shafts from the chinks in the wall, stood the chair, red and shining. The way to it was risky; the floor rocked like ice in the autumn. There was a square hole that had to be avoided too. And the fact that it was such a dangerous place put the English chair out of reach.

The English chair? The very name implied something distant and exclusive. Its bearing was dignified, its back arched and tall, with spindles and turned-out feet; not Windsor, perhaps slightly Rococo, with worn gilding which shone only in strong light. But otherwise red, redder than anyone has ever seen.

We were forbidden to cross the loft. The floor might collapse, and besides — as the grown-ups said — What business would anyone have there?

But the ladder was not forbidden. You could creep cautiously up the six rungs, and get your head above the edge, and look. If you were lucky with the light you could see the English chair as well; it stood far in on the right. In cloudy weather it could only be glimpsed like an ember, but when it was sunny outside and the shafts of light stabbed towards the corner, then the chair flamed like a bonfire, and was unattainably beautiful.

The big boys said someone had sat in it. I had never seen such a thing. Would the floor have been strong enough? But the chair was fascinating not just because it was out of bounds. It was the chair itself. It stood forbidding anyone to approach it. It was attractive and threatening at the same time. It fascinated a poor boy standing with his head sticking up into the loft, and if you were alone you could even talk to it. It dared you to. Sometimes it called out, at length and accusingly. More than one person had heard it. We told each other about it on those silent autumn evenings with darkness between the willows. Perhaps they are standing there still.

Although, I suppose they can't be. For this is another world.

This is a world where objects are clear as daylight, but they have lost their friendliness. Perhaps even willows like that do not whisper together in the autumn evening, when four boys crowd beneath them. At that time they whispered. They had so much to say, and they never said it; they were like us, they were allies. And we knew their secrets, but did not pass them on. And this dark green sea of nettles — it could look black towards evening, and had its terrible secret too. Once a child had fallen into that sea and never returned.

Yes, everything had terror in it and whispered about it. But they were necessary terrors; life was supposed to be dangerous. And it was wrong to tell us there was no danger.

But nobody said that about the English chair. The red colour alone would last for ever. It was a thousand years old, or ten thousand, and English. It was possibly from Africa or further away, and painted with human blood, which was why the colour had lasted so well. And the wood itself came from a tree which doesn't exist on earth any more. Once a queen was tied to the chair, and there she sat until she starved to death, and the worms from the wood hollowed her out while she was still alive. Her screams could be heard all over Africa and far into China. We knew that for sure. There were marks on the seat left by the cavities of the queen's bones, from when she had sat writhing in torment. Then a raven sat on the back of the chair and pecked her eyes out, first one eye and, after a long time, the other, so that she was able to see all the horrors and the beasts that approached her, and the shadows of jackals at the edge of the forest. The jackal is the most cowardly of all animals and waited until she was properly dead. But she saw them with her one eye, and when she screamed, she made the kind of screams that the jackal screams in the night, for that was the sound she heard most often, so she became like a jackal and bayed like a jackal. That queen had been a terrible person; she was English and had only one tooth. It was in her lower jaw and so long that it reached right up to her nose. But some said that when she was dead she would turn into a beautiful princess who had vanished. And sometimes, in the moonlight, the princess came back and sat in the chair, and whoever saw her could wish for anything he wanted. But even the big boys dared not pretend they had seen her. Nor was there anyone who dared pretend that they dared to go near the English chair at night.

We always, always consulted each other under the trees. Their gentle whispering was the undertone to everything we said. And when the wind dropped, we heard another rushing sound, the sea swell breaking over and over again, down on the beach by the cove. The sea could lie black as varnish towards evening, and when the mysterious force reached the cliffs, a muffled boom rose from the ground, and you could feel it in your body.

This was in summertime. One summer Bertram came.

(It had been quiet while Matias Roos was telling his story. But at this moment a change took place. The bartender, who had been standing, sat down and stared at Daniel. The auxiliary, on his part, shrugged his shoulders and adopted an ironic expression, the way people do when they are mentioned and want to affect indifference. Oliver looked up, puzzled, from his cobbler's last, with a youthful, alert expression which altered him completely. The young couple seemed almost alive in their glassy beauty. Only the director sat as before, tired, omniscient.

Matias Roos also stared at Daniel when he mentioned Bertram's name — like a challenge: Yes, I'm coming to you, to your previous name. Has the person changed, the person who bears the name?

He said, 'I recognized you when I saw you in the café, but you slipped away from me, as everything slips away. Not until now did I suspect that everyone meets again.'

Daniel looked shamefaced and tired. 'I suppose I change my name hoping to... Am I the only one?' He got to his feet, his eyes glinting dangerously.

The bartender coughed imperiously: 'Go on!')

Bertram was bigger than we were. His voice had broken already, his jaw was dark with the beginnings of a beard. He took the lead in everything. He was the best swimmer I have ever seen; he was polite to grown-ups and listened to them when they spoke. He lived with relatives. We didn't like him. He sowed seeds of competition which made us uneasy and small. It was no longer important to be good at something; you had to be best. He taught us a gesture: how to shrug our shoulders.

But there was one thing Bertram could not disturb: the English chair. He was more keen to talk about it than anyone. He was daring in everything that he could do better than the rest of us, but he never said he would dare to go into the loft after dark.

One day was warmer and clearer than other days. Oh, those autumn mornings, drenched in dew, glittering and expansive, mornings full of possibilities. The paths in the grass were silver in the green, the smooth rock by the sea glinted with moisture which vanished. The sea fringed itself with minute embroideries of white around the furthest islands.

That day Bertram swam across the sound. Nobody had done that before. He didn't make much of a fuss about it either; the deed spoke for itself. But when he came back to the shore the day seemed to darken. We had talked about the chair the previous evening. He had looked at me then; now he looked at me again. He looked at me each time someone praised his achievement. He had brought *the challenge* among us. What had been a game up to then turned into pressure, into resentment. Neither was our admiration pure; our blue summer had been given a shade of violet. There had been the adult world and our world: two worlds, vigilant, but at peace. With Bertram there came a shadow from that other world, making our own the poorer. He looked at me. I said, 'Tonight I'm going to sit in the English chair.'

I said it without being aware of it, I can swear to that. I was just as horrified as they were. But a desperate joy welled up in me at the same moment. Bertram's evil arts were forgotten, my own small worth forgotten too. And the others? I had taken them with me, lifted them up into a higher sphere, I carried them with me.

The seabirds had gone out to sea that morning, as they sometimes do. Now they returned in flocks, shrieking. And I know that I thought of them as my witnesses, as the boys were my witnesses. But I myself was my worst witness. What was inescapable had arrived. From the flaming sources of self-assertion? Maybe the fuse had been alight for a long time, but I had not noticed the flame — perhaps only as small gusts of pleasure and displeasure like fire and ice.

From that moment I was alone. People smile at that sort of thing. I smile myself; I smile so that the hair rises on my scalp. But I did not smile through the long day that passed after I had said it. Somebody had objected, 'You don't mean that you...' But the words had died away. We stood awkwardly on the rock. The swim across the sound was forgotten, along with all other achievements... And perhaps the idea had occurred to more than one of them, maybe to them all, but they were ashamed of it now and drew away from me. It happens that people see a different person in you than the one you think you are. Thus one changes oneself.

They did not admire me, neither did they doubt me; there are certain things one cannot go back on. They retreated. Children hate misfortune.

Bertram left first. The others' excuses withered on their lips. There was a little boy called Fartein who stayed, and gave me a long stare. Fartein could whistle like any bird; they would come and alight on him. He was a bit of a loner in our company, perhaps possessed of a tenderness that did not wish to give itself away. He stood moving his lips, while his hands busied themselves with something he was holding. Usually it would be a strange root which resembled something else. He always found such things on the beach or in the woods.

I saw that he wanted to say something, and God knows I needed to hear it. I turned away to give him the opportunity, but he must have misunderstood me. When I turned back again I saw only his back and his shoulders, hunched despondently. But he was the only one who stood by me on that occasion, even though he left. It was not the first time I had noticed it.

I had expected to find some of my friends at the woodshed in the twilight, if only to keep me up to it. But nobody was standing by the outhouses, nobody on the narrow path under the alder trees. The clouds had piled up in the course of the day; now they had spread out again. There was a greenish light and it was unusually warm for the time of year.

Up in the house everyone had gone to bed, and the huge red moon that everyone was talking about that autumn no longer lay like a red quilt above the islands at the mouth of the fjord. It had turned into a white button high up, making the leaves glitter like silver. I felt a loneliness that placed me outside myself. As long as I was walking along the path I was outside myself to such a degree that I was not even nervous.

The darkness in the woodshed roused my fear, but it was only ordinary fright, almost pleasant. The smell was the same musty smell as in the daytime. I tripped over the chopping block in the dark. The light from the opening where the ladder was propped up was only like a dull pane of glass, not alarming. I climbed up quickly. I was used to seeing the shafts of sunlight piercing the wall; now they were shafts of moonlight. Everything was different, as if it were floating. I looked carefully at the moon-sharp contours of the mattress and the table frame. I wanted to find out what they looked like in this new light. Then I turned my head towards the furthest object, a red chair.

Seeing it was a shock; I had to cling to the ladder. It was the English chair, but the red looked black in the moonlight. The outline of the chair was so sharp that it seemed quite close, and it was perhaps this sudden nearness that scared me.

I edged my way towards the chair, in sitting position, my back to it. My hands felt the open hole in the floor, so I knew I was going in the right direction. I kept my eyes fixed on the wooden walls; even the planks were not visible except as spaces between the strips of moonlight. But these dark areas were more alive than the staring light; *that* was dead and shining, blue shafts that were fixed inside the room itself, wiping out the difference between in and out of doors. I retreated backwards and away from the dangerous square in order to get away from this blue steel from a sky which was suddenly as limitless in here as out there, where the light itself was floating, lacking perspective. My body felt the cold pain of the stab of the lances. I fled from them and approached the chair, facing it.

Two black soldiers stood before me. They were small and glossy. The one had a shield, the other a sword, and the sword and the shield shone blue in the moonlight. I threw myself down full length, certain that the vision would disappear. But when I glanced up furtively the soldiers were standing there as before. I could not see their expressions, so could not decide whether they were looking at me. But at that moment I realized that I was not as frightened as I would have expected. A vague feeling of delight began to trickle through me. I had reached the terrifying goal.

Then something dragged me towards the chair. Not a mental force which told me that I should creep to it. No, no! Nothing like that. Very much a bodily force which dragged and pulled me, first by the arms and then, when I resisted, by the shoulders. It both pulled and pushed, so that my position became half upright, but at an angle *away* from the chair, struggling with all my might against what was pulling me. And while this was going on I saw the soldiers, who were standing stock still, taking no part in the attack. 'Help me,' I called to them. The small black men seemed to be my allies at that moment. They could have been children dressed up as soldiers.

But the soldiers did not help me. At the same moment I felt all my strength leave me. I did not faint, but a blue mist surrounded me, and when I came to my senses I was sitting in the chair.

My first thought was to get up and run away, but I was unable to move. I was completely lucid at that point. I saw the shining silver moonbeams which turned the mattress green and lay like varnish over the frame of the table. I saw the dust in the strips of light and the thick layer of dust on the floor, a broad track in it left by my body. I was holding the arms of the chair with my hands and was unable to move them, bound as they were. I could not look down; something was holding my neck locked to the curved back of the chair. Only my feet dangled freely.

That was when the fear in me turned white. I knew that I must share the fate of the queen and die in the chair until my joints gnawed into the seat. For the chair was no longer standing in the loft. It was floating in space, in lunar space in an immaterial void where there was neither up nor down. It was a space within space, and it was travelling through space at such speed that the current of air whistled against my face, and I was far away from where the chair had stood and where I lived and where everything was. And this space in space where I found myself was blue and full of light, and the space was filled with beings who approached and retreated with great, rhythmic movements, accompanying the enormous movement of which we were all a part, accommodating themselves to it. Sometimes the creatures were so close that I felt that they were clammy and slippery, but far away in the mist I heard a dog bark, or perhaps a jackal. And the small black soldiers were standing on guard all the time, over the chair, over the person sitting in the chair, the person who — I noticed — was becoming less and less *me*, less and less the person I had been. Slowly there came a being into me. It was not so strange as I first thought; it had visited me before: a being which was full of contempt for what I loved, a being which could only be compared with the timeless adult, the enemy, for whom one minute was just like the previous one and indistinguishable from the next, a being without real life, but with a limitlessness in him. I knew it then: to be an adult is to die. It was the timelessness of the adults which had taken its place in me, the adults' non-relationship to existence — the true fear of mortality, the fear of not being privy to the whole.

Yes, this was what it was to be adult — involved in everything one had created and was responsible for, without any certainty whatsoever of anything at all, bound, bound hand and foot... Astonishing words appeared in space, and they were words like future, shackled, yes shackled! I tugged so sparks flew to free my hands, but they were bound, not by any rope, but by their own will. I felt my blood run cold, because I had wanted this, I wanted it now, and because the promise I had given on the rock had been given in order to escape from everything that was safe and that made no demands on me, on *me*. And I would want it again. I did not regret it.

Yes, yes, I did regret it! I wanted to go back...

The stars in the firmament strode past me, for I was in space! Swallowed up, one with all things, with the stars and the dead, with the terrible queen and two small soldiers with a sword and a shield and with knowledge about those who were to come and with despair on behalf of them all, concern far into infinity for the living and the dead.

I regretted my fourteen years of life, every thoughtless moment, every joy, every night asleep without knowledge of the terrors of space. Singing with the speed, like a star among stars, I heard all the stars singing: space eternally afraid that the creation which had set everything in motion should betray its own laws, and that it would all disintegrate.

But of course it would disintegrate, I knew that now. No more slimy creatures in the mist, no ravens, no empty eye sockets. It would disintegrate, my own self and everything with it. For the balance could not last for ever between such strong forces as these, where the slightest deviation in the ellipses had to lead to catastrophe. Why not sooner rather than later? Why not *my* space against space!

I understood this with words previously unknown to me. It was the message of the willow trees when they whispered towards nightfall; it was the threat of the waves and my own painful longing to be one with everything. Why should only the trees be trees, and not I? And was I never to learn what it was to be water at night and by day, and to groan in dark caves according to the law of the great Will? Oh, the rapture of being all things and of being destroyed with them; of being grass, sea and trees, and seaweed — and wind which fashioned the sea into waves, seaweed rocking in the swell; of being the controller of the winds, a seagull gliding on air; of being able to choose between them, and to choose it all! And to wish! To wish for the extinction of it all, the extinction they carried in their being! To be the forces which controlled and which shattered. Initiator and destroyer. God! God! Let me be everything! Let me be God!

Memory. Agonizing anticlimax. Mother's voice in a room up in the house. 'But why did he want to be there?'
Reply from the door, Fartein's voice. 'Perhaps he had to.'
Mother's voice. '*Had* to, Fartein?'
Fartein: 'I must go now. Please say hello from me when he wakes up.'
Mother's voice: 'But *that* chair? Do you know, Fartein, my grandmother died in that chair. She was killed by a bolt of lightning as she sat in it. She was English.'

Damnable memory that links random events together. The next to arrive was Bertram, tall, well-dressed and polite. I was sitting up by then, with a large hole in my head and some red weals round my wrists that nobody could explain. Hysteria, said the doctor. Doctors do say that sort of thing.
'I didn't even know we had that chair,' said Mother.
Bertram, with a careless air, over a small glass of blackcurrant wine: 'One can't remember everything one collects over the years.'
Poor Mother. There was no explanation to be had.
Nor was there any explanation to give. But for me it was yet another defeat to listen to Bertram sitting there, explaining away something he could not explain: that was adult tactics. *My* lips were sealed with the seal of shame, and with the seal of misgiving. The latter lived in me from that time forward, my enemy.

Silence in the bar.
Peter Gustov, the bartender: 'This Fartein — what happened to

him?'

'He's dead. When he was a student he drowned in five foot of water. Some sailors in a regatta saw him floating face up beneath the surface, but they hadn't the time to save him. They had to get back and win first. Afterwards they turned round and fished up the corpse. He was one of *them*.'

'One of whom?'

'Of those who are killed by competition — others' competition.'

'And this Bertram?' The bartender looked straight ahead. Nothing disclosed that he was interested in Daniel's presence.

'Why do you ask me? He's probably alive. He's that kind.'

The bartender — and he was Peter Gustov now, his true echo: 'The wish. Was it fulfilled?'

'The wish?'

'To be everyone — everything.'

Oliver, his flute in his hand, had left his stool. He walked towards Matias Roos. He had tears in his young eyes.

Matias Roos got to his feet too, and took a step towards him.

'Yes, Fartein. I knew it must be you — in a way. Thank you.'

But before their hands could meet and show their power in the face of all this enmity, the bartender was there again, sharp and imperious: 'Oliver. Your boot.'

Oliver returned to his stool. His expression was snuffed out, as before. He was no longer Fartein, he could not have been, for this man was a humble reflection, no more.

'Your boot, Oliver!' repeated the bartender quietly.

Oliver sat down and began working on the boot.

14

The director said, 'I cannot understand why one should force one's intimate confidences on others. You were asked to tell us a story, and what do you do? Turn your soul inside out and create an embarrassing situation for others.'

Matias Roos noticed the naked hostility around him now.

'I can't remember having asked you for your opinion.'

The director: 'You can't remember me at all. You remember nobody from your environment. As far as you were concerned they were only types in your service. Your fall was accordingly great.'

Bartender: 'Now then!'

'And I, for my part,' answered Matias Roos wearily, 'intend to stick to my right to remember people of your sort as types. All the more because this place seems to have cultivated each person's minimum capacity.'

But he was interrupted by the director's absent-minded expression. The self-satisfied man put on a childishly curious look. He turned enquiringly to the bartender, who reassured him with a low, 'He's coming now.'

Matias Roos: 'Who's coming? Old Buster — the General?'

Bartender: 'Patience!'

'No! I insist on knowing who's coming. I insist on knowing where we are...'

But his energy evaporated as he asked the question. The faces around him bore the features of ironic omniscience. He was the uninvited guest who does not know the rules of the game.

The detective rose and said, turned towards Matias Roos, 'So —

who are *you*, you who hid yourself just now?'
    Matias Roos: 'I'm the wanted person.'
    'Precisely. So that matter's clear.'
    But the detective took no action. The small glimmer of the joy of discovery had slid away from him. His whole being gave the impression of repetition and hopelessness. He listened absent-mindedly to distant sirens.
    The bartender, into vacancy: 'If one could only understand how such fires begin!'
    'Don't be so hypocritical, man!' The detective turned towards him roughly. 'You know everything at least as well as anyone else here. Haven't you been a human being, a destroyer?'
    But this accusation, too, ebbed away into a statement, depriving it of its character of accusation. To Matias Roos he said, 'And you recognize me, I suppose?'
    'Naturally. In your role as prosecutor. Wasn't there someone who called you the Almighty?'
    'Our friend Matias Roos,' said the director, toying with the dice, 'was in fact too busy — I did say *was* — to notice each individual. He took note of us as the initiators of evil.'
    The detective had picked up the dice and was inspecting them absentmindedly. 'But what's this? These dice are fakes! Sixes on every side.'
    The bartender, calmly: 'No matter. They're the Financier's dice. He only plays against himself.'
    The director, somewhat apologetic: 'We only have our two hands. We arrange matters so that we don't actually lose.'
    The detective had acquired that weary expression again when he turned towards Matias Roos.
    'Where you're concerned the case is clear. You admit that you chose everything. That is to say, nothing. The law states that one must be true to one's self.'
    'And the verdict — ?
    'To continue in your choice, I imagine. Always. But I'm not the jury.'
    'You're not apprehending me?'
    'You are apprehended.'

The bartender intervened. 'You were an instrument, was not that so? Not responsible. Your road was short. You're here, after all.'

And he threw out his hand in that ironic gesture of generosity one remembered from a previous time — as if he were demonstrating all the insignificant glories of the world.

'Here?' Matias Roos turned towards the bartender. He felt an echo of the tension that had once been his, the anxiety about everything, the tension about everything. It had decreased from the moment he had entered this room.

'So you may continue your flight,' said the detective coldly. The bartender: '*Here.*'

They laughed. The director laughed with them. Matias Roos felt his energy evaporate, his curiosity disappear; only fragments remained.

'I'd like to ask what that means?'

The question remained hanging in the air. He would have repeated it, but all of a sudden he lost interest. He poured himself a small drink. The bartender went behind the counter and noted it on the board.

Oliver took the flute from his lips and said, 'When I was young music held such a strong attraction for me.'

The bartender came from behind the counter again, still looking at Matias Roos, who shrank from him.

'There is a lack of a sense of permanence.'

He walked right across the room, so that he was standing between the director and Matias Roos. They both cringed under the self-assured voice.

'Permanence,' as I said. Here — ' and the bartender again gestured with his hand in that affected manner they knew so well, 'one learns to have a sense of what is permanent.'

And when nobody answered him: 'Permanence, as I said.'

Matias Roos looked at the door to the street, or to what was outside. He had the choice now. He rose to his feet irresolutely with the sound of the flute in his ears. This apathetic Oliver — was that how he had been? Had it been *his* weakness that he had been incapable of — no, that he had had no desire to fight his way out of a decision, which meant compliance to the point of self-obliteration: an overgrown boy, a caricature of the sweet-natured personality, of all the conciliatory characteristics that had once made such a boy full of potential?

Perhaps he had not drowned on that occasion? Wasn't it precisely — yes, he remembered now — one of those fantasies he had clung to once (so it was true, as the director said, that for him people were only types, personifications); that Fartein was just the type to die on account of the ambition of others. It was as if he, Matias Roos, had recreated the natures of others according to a pattern. *That one* was to win, *that one* to die an early death. The roads were to remain open only for himself. Yes, the roads — they were to divide, always into new roads which created perspectives ready to be seized. He would conquer everything if he so wished and when he wished — a new road when he was tired of the one he was following. As for the victors, they could stand there like dead pathfinders; they had chosen.

He looked towards the door and noticed the bartender watching him. Why not now at this moment — kick over the traces and finish with all these confessions which only burdened him! There was a frontier somewhere. He wanted to reach it, even if it was the last frontier, a place where roads divided no longer.

'*Now* he's coming!' said the director, sweeping up the dice.

The bartender walked over to the barometer and tapped it, without speaking. The door opened. Matias Roos saw at once who it was: the General, Buster whom he had loved once upon a time; the same features, but stiffened; the same expression, but reduced to stupidity through affected harshness. He walked straight into the room and shook the water off his cape.

'Is this the place?' he asked.

The bartender took a couple of paces towards him. 'Yes indeed, sir. Welcome, General!'

The General looked past him. His eye fell on the director.

'Well! So you're here too.'

'As the General can see,' replied the director sarcastically, imitating the bartender's tone of voice.

'Well! And there we have Daniel, the Auxiliary.'

'At your service, General!' Daniel clicked his heels and stood to attention with that little exaggeration which assists the soldier to keep his self-respect.

'And the wretched Oliver.' The General continued his inspection. Oliver nodded and lowered his instrument.

The beautiful young couple danced where they sat. The General shuddered. 'Beautiful youth joins the ranks,' said the woman who had once been called Wenche.

'Patience, General,' said the bartender coldly.

The General: 'Nonsense. Action! What are you laughing at, man?'

But the bartender had swung busily behind the bar to fetch another glass and make a note on the board as the same time. Nothing escaped the general's eye; it seemed applied, as on a portrait in oils.

'What were you doing at the board?' He sipped his drink.

'Noting it down, General. Matter of routine. Would the General be kind enough to make a note of his consumption himself?'

'There'll be no consumption here. I do not intend to stay here, idle.'

He looked around him in the half-dark bar. 'And the name of this place is — ?'

'As you saw on the signboard, General.'

The general said, full of disdain, '*No Man's Land*. What's that supposed to mean?'

'I'm sure the General knows. Or perhaps one of the gentlemen ...'

'I'm asking you in order to get an answer,' said the general curtly. But he looked about him, at the director, at the young couple, at Daniel. Matias Roos tried to catch his eye; he tried to capture an inkling of their past friendship. He no longer felt surprise.

The general's gaze remained with the director.

'So you still play?'

'Only against himself,' said the bartender quickly. 'Only against himself!' The general: 'Against himself? But then he has no opponent, nobody who loses!'

The director shrugged his shoulders. But the general advanced to the attack. 'What the devil is this place? You used to be a man of probity, a man who insisted on justice for himself!'

Nobody answered him. He looked about him. The swish of the

rain grew louder.

'No Man's Land?' pondered the general.

The bartender was standing close beside him, a little too close for a bartender.

'We hope you'll feel at home. You're free to do business here too. To do business. And where credit is concerned...'

'I haven't asked for credit!'

Oliver began playing again. The bartender went behind the counter.

'I'll serve the General a chop.'

But the general rose abruptly. 'I'm *not* staying here!' he announced.

His glance fell on the barometer. He repeated, but with slightly less energy, 'I'm not staying here.' He turned towards the room and studied them all. For an instant Matias Roos recognized Old Buster behind the stern demeanour. His instinct was to approach him, to offer him his hand. But the general remained standing, his gaze empty. 'No, I am *not* staying — here.'

The bartender came out with a tray balanced on the palm of one hand and cutlery in the other.

'Gentlemen, it's getting dark.'

The general sat down heavily, his back to the director. He looked at the barometer. 'Change!'

The bartender put a cloth on the table. 'That's the only thing that does change here.' He removed the lid of the small tureen.

The general read the lettering on the gallery. '*Paradise* — ?'

'As you see, General, there are women here too.' He arranged a plate and the cutlery.

The general leaned back slightly, his gaze falling on Matias Roos. He nodded slowly, as if something was beginning to dawn on him.

'That too. Of course — at the place where everything continues.'

'Women, as I said,' commented the bartender. '*One* woman, to be precise. Whose turn is it? — Well, it's true she has only one breast.'

The general recoiled. The woman appeared on the gallery for a moment. Matias Roos followed everybody's gaze. He had known about this, too. He felt the general's gaze on himself and met it. And it was as if this gaze was lifted out of the face from which it came, a gaze that was alone in the world, so full of pain that nobody owned it any more, a gaze — not from where pain dwelt, but which was pain itself.

The general's head sank heavily to the table.

'That too,' he murmured.

Matias Roos went towards him, wishing to say something, to call something back.

But the bartender came between them. He smoothed the tablecloth and said, 'Dinner is served!'

15

And not until that moment — when the fat bartender said, 'Dinner is served!' — did Matias Roos understand anything about his life.

He had not lived it. He had experienced more than most — so he had thought. But he had not lived his life, not for an instant.

Voices came to him, from the cool conversations under the willow trees, from the philosophical dinners with powerful men, from bars and from bedsides. One voice said, 'What an infantile mind. Who told you the lie that it is important to make sacrifices?'

Other voices, a single one: 'Sacrifice, even if only one — that's what's important.'

And yet another: 'Temptation resisted? Uncommitted sin, ha ha!'

Mother's voice, reading aloud in the evening: 'And then the boy gave his jacket to the stone so that it shouldn't feel cold...'

The voices of the children round the plate of sandwiches:

'What a silly boy!'

'What a silly boy!'

'What a silly boy!'

But Fartein's frail voice made itself heard through the din:

'Perhaps he had to.'

He was surrounded by cloud. Thick mist came down from dark mountains and attempted to enclose him in indecisiveness. He flailed his arms in order to free himself. He had lived in these mists. And each time gleams of light from outside had built a bridge towards a way out, he had walked on that bridge. 'We've been given our two eyes in order to see our chances, after all. We've been given our two hands in order to...'

He stood among these recollections of human beings, and said softly:

'I'm asking about human feeling itself — how our minds change. With what right can we know that everything takes place in one and the same person? Can we assume it at all? We take it for granted that a self is a self. We give it names and all the signs and establish a postulate, until we believe we can't free ourselves of it: a point of departure, and certain, fixed limits. But is this true?'

They looked at him without answering.

'The roads. All the roads — !'

Someone laughed softly in the dark.

All the thousands of roads that had become his, because he had walked along them!

Were they whispering together? They were not going to let him move forward...

He had known it — all the roads had only been means of escape. The true roads — perhaps *they* knew them, those responsible men he had met, those men with knowing expressions, those who had said, 'Matias Roos will never grow up.'

There had been a road he believed in, the one that led to the frontier without dividing. What had happened? The papers... an official had said they were not valid, they were of no significance?

Naturally. The official had known, the faceless man in uniform. The identity card? Who can have a card showing his own identity? A piece of cardboard for folding up, with a picture of a face. Height, hair, eyes, age. Hair and height and two brown shoes which had become down at heel on their way towards a frontier. The official had not looked at him, hadn't compared him with the card. He had known that a human being cannot be folded up for ever, and say, 'That's me.' A human being cannot for ever be the model with whom such a card is matched.

Yes, the model. He looked at the beautiful couple in the weak light of the bar. Models. Models of human beings. The general, the director: models who had continued their lives as models. Time had caricatured them, *until they matched.*

'Can this be the substance of a beautiful word: Eternity?'

The detective, a custodian with no conscience other than that everyone must conform to the plan — his plan! It had led Daniel astray; he became a grown man, he twisted and turned as the solution dictated.

He looked at them now; they looked back, wondering in their darkness where they found themselves.

Oliver! — No, not that Fartein who had wanted to console him on the rocks by the fjord. Can one bore through a soul with a cobbler's awl? Live and let live, they said. *Kill* and let live! The Fartein who had wanted to take his burdens from him was no longer alive. He went his way on that occasion. The others left, it's true. But Fartein left as well. There had been a rough design for a Fartein, the same design as for Matias Roos. The real Fartein, the one who ought to have been Fartein, would have stayed, would have known about the English chair and shared its dangers with him, the danger of travelling to the land and riches of hearts' desire, so full of horror and of all that a soul can long for. But Fartein had left, he had drowned. Or not drowned. He had been seen in five foot of water with his eyes open. He had been alive beneath the water. But nobody had had time to pick him up then; his screams had been smothered by water. Whether it was truth or falsehood that he had drowned, he was dead in his mould.

But perhaps a human being's goodwill lives on — lives on under water.

'When I was young music held such a strong attraction for me.'

He was standing in the centre of the room now, facing a door, the eyes of those who dreaded their eternity upon him. He could shout his fearless protest in their faces, and die, or be annulled as a link in the company of the living dead:

'Play then, Oliver! Play Fartein back. His pattern was to be affectionate and kind. Play this bartender and his models in to their eternity. Play them deep into No Man's Land where they all belong. Play, Fartein!'

But Fartein humbly picks up his boot from the floor; he plays only in defiance, to pretend he exists.

'Oh, Fartein, Oliver — dear child with many names, play so that walls collapse into rubble, you who possess the gift of gentleness. Be bold in your humility. Even cowardice demands courage. Be Fartein, choose that! Then you will live! Don't be shy because you are Fartein, but fear the shyness that hides behind a bold front. That's how shy you must be!

You must not defeat anyone. You must allow your design to develop; it must not become a model! You must grow in the mould in which you were created. You knew that once. When did you cease to know it?

Murder me, burn me — me, Matias Roos. Cut into my flesh, scatter my entrails and let my eyes sprout into a vision, of ravens' excrement. Cut into my flesh and rupture my heart, my heart! But let his heart be caressed by a dove's wing...

Childhood, childhood, lost land — may he win it back!'

III

16

She sat in silence for a long time. His gaze had been in another world. Now it became slowly kindled by the present, but he did not meet her eyes. Her fingers were tracing the pattern of the plastic table top.

'And how much of this is reality?'

'The trouble with reality is that it depends on — on belief. You're saying that I never met these people again?'

'This Fartein — *did* he drown?'

'I don't know. With the best will in the world I can't say I know! I've never told you that I play the flute?'

She shuddered.

'Didn't he keep your mother company that time you came round after the English chair?'

He covered her cold hands with his.

'I suppose you think I've dreamt it all. Has it never occurred to you that there might be twins of different mothers?'

'Fartein went astray too, in his way.'

'He lies under water. Now and again I can hear him calling.'

She warmed her cold hands in his, which were fever-hot. She said, 'And this No Man's Land?'

'A concept from the Reformation in Scandinavia. A place where human beings travel between life and death in a kind of extended caricature of life.'

'Somewhat like Mrs Skarseth's marriage?' She laughed briefly.

'Like very many human lives. Like those lives that I met. Like all that is terrifying.'

'Like *your* life? Fleeing from the flight that always continues? No, no, don't answer me, I'm trying to understand. You wanted to hide your true Self for fear of — and then it broke out. But the fear...! You said once that you were an old man. Or you thought it. It was in the avenue. I guessed that you thought so. It hadn't occurred to me.'

'Now it does occur to you. Maybe age doesn't become reality until you talk about it. In the avenue I was thinking that no one could love an old man; no one could begin to love him.'

'But yes,' she said.

He looked at her for the first time after a long interval. He said, 'The young are afraid as well, but not all the time, and they are reluctant to admit it. They want to keep their belief that they're one, one single human being. You become old when you give up that belief and know it, when you have to admit the independence of your guilty Self, when you can no longer deny your straying Ego.'

'*Something* good happened to your Matias. He got away. He wasn't just a victim.'

'All his efforts cost others their lives and happiness, isn't that enough? Every acknowledgement of guilt is retrospective in its effect.'

'Do you remember our comic philanthropist that time we met at the lecture? Perhaps to a certain extent he was right in saying that they didn't know. His young Theodore — do you remember him? That they don't know...'

'Surely the problem is that we *must* know. It's as simple as that.'

It was evening when they left the cafeteria, and they had been awake a whole night.

I, who stay in the House, feel we have never been so close since he decided to leave, and stood in the sun. But he doesn't seem relieved as he walks beside her. Although they're holding hands they feel it's a little silly. Perhaps all the concern she has shown him is weighing on him now. He doesn't completely believe in her as the strong one of the two. Her perception is much too sensitive for that. She absorbs things too strongly. In the avenue last night she was one with his shyness.

And now, as they stand in the street outside Mrs Skarseth's home for the homeless, now the house itself appears homeless in the cold evening light. And she says at once, 'It looks as if something's happened.'

They both look up at the second floor with its old-fashioned starched curtains, its indestructible plants which always hover between life and death at this time of year.

He glances at her questioningly. She nods.

Then they climb up the long flight of stairs together and she unlocks the door to let him in.

An unfamiliar coat is hanging in the narrow cloakroom, a worn, unattractive garment in an indistinct shade of blue.

'Johanna has come,' she says.

17

'Johanna has come,' said Mrs Skarseth.

She appeared in the entrance hall just as they were about to sneak past. They looked at her, and the one knew that the other was also thinking that she had become an old lady. ('Was that what *she* thought about *me* when she finally raised her eyes in the cafeteria?')

Mrs Skarseth beckoned them into the hall. 'I have a special little meal for you in there, a bottle of Chianti too — no, she's not there, let's sit down for a moment. I'm happy to have my daughter back, even though it's only for a short time. But I don't know, perhaps she won't... Johanna has never said anything about her plans. Her luggage... what was I saying? Happy. Nowadays these independent women — you're not worried about them. It's not like the old days when they were a perpetual burden, a source of concern. Mr Roos, you look concerned yourself, older — oh, I'm sure you'll forgive me, perhaps I'm a little upset. Our Sonja is fortunately as fresh as a daisy, that does me good. I'd rather have unconcerned people in my house, good-natured people. There's so much unpleasantness in the world, one of my guests is being questioned today; his residence permit... Oh, isn't it dreadful how many papers people need all the time, can you understand it? Papers east and west. Who are we when all's said and done? All this proof makes one thoroughly confused. We are who we are, isn't that so, Mr Roos? One paper more or less, a name, a description — even a person's appearance changes, after all, as the years, as the minutes go by when time passes like an avalanche. My husband always said, "One must be able to prove one's identity." And what of it? What can anyone prove? But he was a military man, used to numbers. So my daughter has come home. She stood in front of me. Johanna! I said. Oh, but she's so shy. She finds it difficult to show her feelings. I want to embrace her, she just stands there. And I stand there. We mustn't force ourselves on our children. Imagine, children! A grown woman, with responsibilities, adviser to children and young people, so much more than I ever achieved. Mother, she says. Oh well, perhaps she doesn't say that exactly. But her expression — oh, once upon a time I held a little one like that on my knee. The years pass, I don't know. Often they don't seem to pass at all. Then all the years pass in an instant. I didn't know what to do with my hands, with these hands, they have held so much. Have you thought about that — everything our hands have held? The same hands that have smashed a dish in anger have caressed a man's body, the same man who was the source of that anger. What a strange life, even the simplest — even mine — many lives. If only someone could find a connection, it's as if the seconds are meaningless, the hours, well, well, but in the long run, or perhaps when we finally look back, when we have time, I don't know. But she didn't want anything to eat. And indeed, why should we always be offering food? Why should a mother —? So, she won't eat. Besides, I have an empty room, that doesn't happen often, but she couldn't know that, of course, she wasn't a bit surprised. She's there now, I think she's there, she wanted to rest. She carried up her luggage herself, two suitcases. But she left this one behind, forgot it on the floor, a shopping bag, open as you see. An envelope had fallen out of the bag, some papers slid out of the envelope, I collected them, they lay there open, just as they're lying now, although I've pushed them together a little, only a little, so she won't be suspicious. But I couldn't help seeing the papers, one or two of them; it's correspondence between her and the education authorities, with her copies included. There's been a difference of opinion, she's been dismissed, she's been accused of absenting herself from her job, of drinking, of having been drunk in class. There are other accusations as well. I've known my daughter for — many years. People accuse her, she defends herself. Or, rather, she doesn't really defend herself, she counterattacks. I insist, it's not my habit to read people's letters. In this house people show me letters, and sometimes more of them than is good — for me. I don't need to read other folks' letters, but they slid out, and she *is* my daughter, it took me twenty hours to give birth to her, and still they had to do a caesarian, what was I saying, she attacks in turn, she accuses the school board of corruption and one of its members of an attempt to rape her in her isolated house up there under the midnight sun. What is one to believe? So much happens, anything is possible. I stood with these papers in my hands, the one after the other, I didn't want to read them, didn't want to know. But what can one do, I ask you? Before you can turn round you know more than you want, yet less than you're compelled to want to know. What do I want? Not this, at any rate. Nobody wants to know everything about their fellow human beings, about their children. But before you can turn round, you know. What then? You close your eyes, your brain, you close yourself entirely and say: I don't know about it. Not I. But you do know. She accuses the school board of negligence, of persecution. She accuses them of persecuting her because she has a child. Her private life is investigated, her unhappy childhood. Things appear in a different light. Where do they come from — herself? Things can be seen in so many different ways, can be said in so many ways. Perhaps her childhood *was* unhappy. Her father drank, it's true. But there's nothing there about that. Her mother — you can read about a person, can't you, in the newspaper for instance. All of a sudden I realize that this is myself. Things can be written there... but it's not me. Not as I've understood it. Like others — ? What others? Or like a third or a fourth. What can people possibly know? A person has many faces. Her mother ran an establishment, it says. Beaulieu. They must mean Beaulieu. But the word itself becomes an insinuation. The child, it says, heard music and singing till the small hours. The songs at the wedding parties! Oh, those wedding songs that robbed me of all my courage. They write about strangers, they came and went. About refugees with many names, about visits from the police, what of it? Aren't the police everywhere? No, no, I'm not going to defend myself, not against you two, it's not necessary. Everything can be seen from two sides, from ten sides. You start to doubt, to think back. Everything appears in an uncertain light, reflected. You appear in a shifting light yourself. You can't see your own face. Yes, the police *were* here, today, it was about Esterhazy,

he's stolen something at his place of work. He stole a little from me too, a few spoons. I noticed it at once. I said, "Esterhazy, those spoons." He brought them to me at once. He was like a frightened animal, he's lived in camps, I would have stolen too. Wouldn't you have stolen, Mr Roos?'
'I would have stolen.'
'I knew it. I knew I could rely on you. There are limits to our morality, and that limit is reached quite soon. My husband was so honest he wouldn't pick up a halfpenny in the street. But he used up all that I earned unless I kept an eye on him. I'm not complaining. People are different, but he was very honest, he couldn't stand lies, he would say, "Antoinette, this guest or that guest of yours hasn't paid any rent for three months." I would say yes he has. He would say no. I would say, what does it matter? He would say he couldn't stand a liar, why didn't I throw the person out? He had very high self-esteem, the Colonel. My daughter has very high self-esteem. She gets it from her father. It's a question of income, of so much else. And besides, drinking? People find it so easy to say a woman drinks, especially if she has a child. A man... Oh well, I'm broad-minded. Why shouldn't he drink? It made him feel good. Or not good. He lived, his time passed. Johanna — she's had to put up with so much, she came to a country, a foreign country, one might say. I ask you again, Mr Roos, wouldn't you have drunk?
'I would have drunk.'
'I told Sonja so, he's a gentleman, I said. Besides, a malicious child in a classroom can say so many things. They get to the ear of the school board, a whole district-full of adulterers and drinkers and tax-evaders, and they unload their guilt on to a stranger, a woman who in addition has a child — *one* child, you notice. One blot on your reputation is halved if there are two, and if there are several it disappears altogether. Johanna drinks? Why shouldn't she drink if she wants to? I've never enjoyed it myself, there's been so much else, but everyone has her own inclinations. I had a German living here who wore ladies' underwear, I laundered it, what of it? He gave my canary hemp seed out of the goodness of his heart, it gave it constipation and killed it, but he meant well, he took guinea pigs to bed. There are all sorts in this world, we don't meet them all, we don't understand

them, we don't understand our own children and the children don't understand their parents. Antoinette, I can say to my reflection, and when I see my lips forming the vowels I think someone else is saying it, that it's a stranger's face, a different mouth. I think, someone is talking to you, the world is as it used to be. Should I be concerned about this trifle? If only Johanna had mentioned it herself. It's unpleasant to make a discovery against the will of the person who's exposed, you're left with a guilty conscience. I don't doubt that Johanna can deal with her little misunderstandings, but she's aggressive, she's touchy about her self-esteem, like her father. Events repeat themselves. Sometimes I ask myself, are we all repeats? Don't we pass through life more and more like shadows, first of ourselves, then of the shadow? Our individuality — where does it go? It turns into a caricature. I, Antoinette Skarseth, must have been somebody once, unique. Johanna — and this is what worries me a little — seems like a caricature, a simplification perhaps. What is left? Bigotry. And what is left of me? Dutifulness, a caricature of dutifulness and caring that can even be seen through. An echo all my life perhaps, for all I know. In that case so be it; we'll manage, as long as we don't brood on it. Good heavens, there are no limits to what we find to talk about. And here I sit, keeping you, while your supper's getting cold. Quick, go along in, forget what I've said. The wine is opened.'

She laughed hurriedly. Then she wept, briefly and violently, but soon got to her feet with a stony expression. The brooch heaved on her well-rounded bosom.

As she stood in front of them, she was no longer an old woman, but a tigress prepared to defend her young.

Sonja threw her arms round her neck, and led her to a chair. A mother too, he thought — or a caricature of a mother.

18

These persons — did they concern me? I am alive and in the House in the forest; I never doubted that I was right. For the decision on that morning pregnant with light did not bring good fortune.

Misfortune. Could I have averted it? His part of our whole was too strong. It happened while he was standing on the crest of the hill, spun about with light, the morning his plans began to dominate, with their unfortunate continuation.

Afterwards it all happened quickly. He would have nothing of *myself*. He deprived me of his company, became wrapped up in that of others, perhaps because he found a confirmation of all his unfortunate experience in the words of this energetic woman. For Mrs Skarseth has an extraordinary strength. Her confused experience pulls her in one direction, as if it occurs according to her needs. It seems as if human beings are ambiguous about everything, yet all of a sudden they can become straightforward, as if in a kind of irradiation from a listener, from the person they're playing to. As Sonja says, 'Mrs Skarseth has never drawn conclusions before. It's as if she had been with us in the cafeteria.'

It all happened quickly. The arrest. His thoughts did not reach me, but isolated themselves in a terrible desire for destruction, as when the magistrate asked, 'So you deny none of this?' And he replied, 'I deny nothing.'

It was the same night, his second night awake. During the judge's summing up he seemed as if turned to stone, and they both seemed turned to stone rather than terror-stricken. And that it should have been Mrs Skarseth's evidence that condemned him — against her will, against her will, against her will. In the end she could say nothing else.

The Judge: 'I shall now recapitulate this preliminary hearing. I request those present to express their objections during the deposition, so that everything can be clarified'.

'At 23.55 hours the owner of the boarding house, Mrs Antoinette Skarseth, 68 years of age, hears her lodger, Katrine Kaas, 32 years of age, who calls herself Sonja and will be called by this name in what follows, leave the table where she had been eating supper with her friend, whose name is given as Matias Roos, 56 years of age, previously convicted, while the latter clearly remains sitting at table. It is stated that Mrs Skarseth heard this, not with any intention of listening, but solely because it was nearly midnight, the time when she normally goes the rounds of the corridors and public rooms. This is also the reason why Mrs Skarseth can give the time so precisely. Mrs Skarseth does *not* go into the dining room, however, so as not to seem obtrusive. She is half expecting the said Matias Roos to come out into the hall to take his leave. On the other hand, she has no objection to his not doing so, if he intends to visit Sonja in her room instead. It is stated that, while waiting, Mrs Skarseth sits looking at old letters and photographs, the latter dating from her daughter Johanna's childhood. Somewhat later, probably at 0.30 hours, she nevertheless goes into the dining room and finds it empty. Plates and glasses have been cleared from the table, which makes it possible to assume that Mrs Skarseth has dozed for a while over her photographs in the hall, since she has heard no sound from the dining room. She walks about the rooms for a while, clearing away, makes sure the front door is locked, notices that Matias Roos's outer clothing is nowhere to be seen, but remembers that he never used an overcoat, and always went bare-headed. Now she goes towards Sonja's room, not — as she explicitly insists — out of any kind of curiosity, but because it was her habit to listen at the door to see whether Sonja was asleep, and sometimes to give in to the temptation to draw the blanket over her. It also happened that she kissed her hair. (Mrs

Skarseth weeps uncontrollably during this part of the deposition.) At the door she hears no sound. Mrs Skarseth has extraordinarily acute hearing and is, as has been explained, used to listening for Sonja's breathing. She then opens the door. It is almost dark in the room, no lamp is switched on, but a little light is filtering in from the street. She sees a figure rise from the bed and immediately recognizes Matias Roos, noticing that he is very pale. They stand facing one another, neither utters a word. Mrs Skarseth's intention is to leave, as she does not wish to disturb an intimate situation. But Roos makes a gesture that prevents her. She then goes to the bed and sees that Sonja is lying with her head flat against the sheet, while the pillow has fallen to the floor. She now also notices that the face of the recumbent woman has a curious colour ("like a dark shadow", as she expresses it). Matias Roos, who is still standing beside the bed, says, "Sonja is dead. Phone the doctor, phone the police." Mrs Skarseth cannot tear her eyes away from Sonja's face; she nevertheless notices that Roos's hands are trembling violently. Then she runs out to the hall and telephones the doctor (who arrived within ten minutes and established that death had occurred round about midnight, caused by suffocation, probably by means of the pillow, the one lying on the floor.) Roos repeats that she must notify the police, but Mrs Skarseth is reluctant to do so. At this point, and in spite of the doctor's statement, she does not quite realize that Sonja is dead. Her refusal, according to her explanation, is due to "a kind of paralysis". ("She was like a daughter to me; sometimes more than my own daughter.") Therefore Roos himself goes out into the hall and phones the police (who arrived shortly after the doctor had undertaken his investigation; it should be added that the doctor had asked whether the police had been notified). However, by now the time is 0.55 hours. At 1.05 hours the room is sealed. Mrs Skarseth and Matias Roos consent to be driven to the police station for a preliminary interrogation. The apartment is placed under police surveillance during Mrs Skarseth's absence. The preliminary interrogation results in the detention of the aforementioned Matias Roos, while Mrs Skarseth is given permission to return home. The indictment against Matias Roos will be drawn up on the basis of this interrogation.'

Mrs Skarseth: 'Against my will, against my will, against my will.'

'Why don't you tell them?'

I stand with my head against the grey and red log wall while this is going on, trying to conjure up a solution. And in the time that followed... I stand with my head against the wall, knocking it against the wall from time to time, saying, Why don't you tell them? Shall I come and save you? Why don't you tell them that it was somebody else?

But it's as if his independent will is too strong. It paralyses me, this desperate urge to — no no no, he doesn't mention the word, doesn't think it. It occurs on my side of the divide: *atonement*. And his favourite expression at one time: bygone days. Everything is culminating now. Evil, something tells him, does not rest. But I say to the wall in the forest that it depends on whether one leaves it alone, on whether one leaves everything alone.

But he says: Nothing rests, everything continues. Something tells him that this unfortunate activity is a part of a condition, something that exists. Something tells him that the interval that has just taken place was only an interval. This voice tells him that he knows it now. Everything in his life has been such a 'now'. With every 'now' he thought himself to be wiser, closer to what he calls truth, which does not exist, but which he will never give up believing in...

Does he, then, simply want to believe that he can be punished retrospectively and so find his childhood again, the childhood he cherishes like a dreamlike state within himself?

If so, then he is lost, lost once more. Nobody becomes a child again, nobody becomes whole; one can come close to one's Self and reduce the tension, reduce it from what is unendurable to what can be endured — and continue to live, that is all. Is there anything else I demand of him, of my Self? No, I do not demand, I beg him from the walls in the green-painted cell: it's not a bad alternative. Green... perhaps to convey hope, or to bestow calm. But he is not calm, he shirks it and will not allow me to know about it.

In court he appears to be calm. The newspapers write that he shows no contrition — he who was already contrite *before*... before everything. The experts talk of apathy, they know all about it.

Cynicism, write the newspapers. People are trying to help him, they are humane, but he will have none of it, they write.

He says nothing about 'bygone days'. Only Sonja knows about that and she's dead. Even she knows it only in the version which perhaps is fiction — *he* doesn't know, after all! For what is fiction when you tell your own story, about that part of the Self which never gets further than to be an echo of an imaginary condition; no no no, I'm being unjust now — not an imaginary, but a possible condition, a longing for innocence!

'The motive,' I whisper. I am whispering to Counsel for the Defence. I see him nodding. He will come to that...

Counsel for the Defence: 'You were very fond of the deceased? You were in love with her?'

Defendant: 'I was very fond of her.'

Counsel for the Prosecution: 'You had a relationship with her?'

Counsel for the Defence: 'My Lord, I find the question irrelevant.'

Defendant: 'I have no objection to replying. I had no relationship with her.'

Counsel for the Prosecution: 'You were, as they say, emancipated persons. Was there any special reason for this reticence?'

Defendant: 'Yes, one reason. An emotional reason.'

Judge: 'Can the defendant describe in more detail the emotional relationship between the deceased and himself?'

Defendant (remains silent).

Counsel for the Defence: 'Will the defendant tell us once again exactly what happened after he left the table?'

Defendant: 'I walked across the passage, knocked at the door.'

Counsel for the Defence: 'You knocked at the door of her room. There was no reply. Had you an agreement to go to her room?'

Defendant: 'There was no agreement.'

Counsel for the Defence: 'You had said good night?'

Defendant: 'We had said good night.'

Counsel for the Defence: 'An impulse, then? Had there been any disagreement?'

Defendant: 'No disagreement.'

Counsel for the Prosecution: 'You had been together for a very long time, the whole day, the previous night. What did you talk about all that time?'
Defendant: 'About certain experiences that affected our lives.'
Counsel for the Prosecution: 'Your life, you mean?'
Defendant: 'My life, yes. It concerned her.'
Counsel for the Prosecution: 'And may I be permitted to ask what these experiences were?'
Defendant (remains silent).
Counsel for the Defence: 'Had you in any way expressed a pessimistic attitude to life that could have affected her, so that — '
Counsel for the Prosecution: 'We have the evidence of the experts that there is no known example of a person successfully using a pillow for the purpose of suicide.'
Judge: 'There is no possibility of suicide. So when you opened the door into the room...?'
Defendant (remains silent).
Counsel for the Prosecution: 'Is this persistent silence on this point to be interpreted to mean that you do not remember what happened?'
Counsel for the Defence: 'The defendant has never asserted that he did not remember. Are you aware that refusal to explain what happened can lead to — misunderstanding? If you could tell us — '
Counsel for the Prosecution: 'The police have worked on this point for months. Among other things he has been asked whether there was anyone else in the room.'
Counsel for the Defence: 'Was there anyone else in the room?'
Defendant (remains silent).
Counsel for the Defence: 'Are you shielding someone? One of the boarders?'
Defendant: 'I would rather be sentenced.'

From the newspapers:
The court was adjourned. The defendant was led away. He appeared absent-minded, but not lethargic. His obstinate refusal to express an opinion on the very moment of the murder would seem to indicate that he does not wish to exclude the possibility of his shielding someone, while

on the other hand, in the opinion of the police, there is not the slightest possibility that another person could have forced his way into the room, just as there is no shadow of a motive on the part of any of those who might possibly be considered. The eight boarders in the establishment lived in the section of the apartment that was furthest away. Neither does the tendency of the Counsel for the Defence to envelop the decisive part of the action in mystery seem to be able to obscure the most obvious conclusion as to what has occurred...

... and knock my head on the log wall here, where there's a smell of peeling paint in the sun, where there's a smell of peace... and call silently, can't they see, even though he says nothing, can't they listen to the silent lie? Or at least accept as an admission what is meant as an admission? For he is incapable of lying now, of lying directly and saying he did it. He cannot say, 'The room was empty.' He cannot say that. Even though he wishes to be sentenced, he cannot contribute to it with a barefaced lie, because it seems to him that the lie will increase the guilt that rests on him, *in* him, so that life will be too short to atone for it all. Even if it's his last naive action in this life, it is at any rate genuine: that something *can* be atoned for. So let him remain in that belief. Sentence him! Sentence him! Or will the jury be unable to sleep? Doesn't the public sense of justice also have a claim to rest? Sentence him!

But a voice in me also says: Don't sentence him! He longed to be back here even before he left, because a part of his mind was in flight. It was in flight towards decisions, even if they were to lead to destruction. And if it's true that that's what he was longing for — then, what of it? Doesn't the survivor always think that maybe it's best that way? Doesn't the survivor think it in self-defence? And that part of him which is 'the survivor' in this house in the forest between a large and a small lake, doesn't that part think so too? Don't 'I' think so? I think like Mrs Skarseth: against my will...

His mind swings between contrary possibilities. He could, after all, answer one or two of these questions, which go on pounding in him between the walls of his cell after every cross-examination.

'Will the defendant tell us what happened when he entered the

room?'
'Was there anyone in the room when you arrived?'
'When you went over to the bed — was Sonja dead at that point?'
'Did you seize the pillow?'
'Did anyone leave the room while you were there?'
'Did you hear anyone enter the room while you were sitting at table?'
'Are you shielding somebody?... Are you shielding somebody?... Are you shielding somebody?...'

And to Mrs Skarseth: 'Is there anyone you have reason to suspect as having had a grudge against the deceased?'

Yes, because he must know. After all, I know, I who am so close to him, I know with that part of him which is longing to be back in the house in the forest, to that uneventfulness that he wished to leave, but of which he wants to be a part. Is, then, his urge to be sentenced so strong that he has used all his powers of the imagination negatively: in order to forget? I whisper to you across all the distances that you only have to tell the truth. Then you will be free as a bird from that moment. But you whisper back to me: The truth. What is it? Was it the truth when they gave me my freedom after the killing of a child? And I whisper as firmly as I possibly can that you didn't kill a child, you saw a sleeveless garment, you can't even say that your hidden purpose... for your hidden purpose is not the same as the guilt you burdened yourself with, which you have burdened *us* with in advance, the guilt we sought peace from in that complete uneventfulness in the forest.

I whisper across all the distances: Tell them, tell them exactly what happened. You have no need to shield *her*; you don't even know her. Johanna is a stranger to you.

And you answer that all this about shielding — has nothing to do with the case.

Correct. It has nothing to do with the case. You say that, if it is to be said, someone else must say it. But does Mrs Skarseth know? Has she any suspicion? It may not have occurred to her. Perhaps she is protected by the law of self-defence and is not allowing herself to admit it? Precisely. And she cannot glimpse a shadow of a motive.

Not for an instant in all these years has it occurred to her that a narrow-minded, harassed little teacher up in the far north has been tormented by filial jealousy, year out and year in, through the dark winters and in the far too light summers which have exposed her increasing age and diminishing charm; and that this tormented soul has turned against her mother in hatred and fury because certain platitudes concerning liberty and outdated prejudices have had the effect of leading her into an aggressive stance she never, in the depth of her heart, wished to assume; that there were times when she could have killed her child; that there were times when she wanted to kill herself, to kill her mother, but that her hatred came to focus on this Sonja, described with affection in so many letters: this stranger (so good-natured, so beautiful, so self-sacrificial!) on whom all her sick jealousy came to focus, in a multitude of emotions which grew progressively more hostile, progressively more militant — this young woman who had been successful in everything a 'liberated' daughter ought to have succeeded in, and yet had not been left saddled with a child.

Mrs Skarseth will not admit it. Her sixty-eight-year-old instinct for self-preservation is like reinforced concrete, reinforced a little more with every year of drudgery and struggle that has passed in her caricature of a life, a woman who knows more than the Lord's Prayer, but on the other hand has forgotten even that. Perhaps because she has repeated the one prayer about our daily bread for so long: Give us.

And by this 'us' she has meant more than herself. She has included her guests, as she calls them, and Sonja, this Sonja above all, and finally her paramour, is that not so?

The court will not admit it. The investigators — have they overlooked the possibility? Well, the defendant himself does not say that anyone was in the room, the defendant merely reveals himself, the defendant mystified the simple facts with sudden silences at decisive moments. He does not reply when he is asked, 'Was anyone in the room when you went in?' 'Did anyone answer when you knocked at the door?'

He does not reply, 'No, nobody said "Come in".' He does not reply, 'When I opened the door I saw a woman leaning over the bed — no not leaning, she had been leaning over it. What I saw was that she moved quickly from the bed towards the window, and from there to the furthest corner of the room, perhaps so as not to stand silhouetted against the light from the street. But I was able to see her face. It had an expression of hatred and pain. She was a large woman. I had never seen her before, but I recognized her from pictures shown me by Mrs Skarseth. She was Johanna, Mrs Skarseth's daughter; she had come home that day. I hurried towards the bed. I suspected — no, I knew what had happened. I even knew the motive at the same instant. I could see it all so clearly, so clearly that a pang of self-reproach went through me because I had not guessed what might happen. I had seen through Mrs Skarseth's calm attitude towards her daughter long ago. To top it all, she had even given herself away completely only — Good God, it had been an hour ago, or a little more. I ought to have guessed, thought, known... all this hurtled through me as I threw myself on the bed, together with a hope, a desperate hope that I had not come too late. I snatched the pillow away and saw her face. I put my mouth on hers and tried to fill her lungs with air, with air from my lungs. I heard the figure over in the corner move, creep out, then was gone. But I didn't hear anyone come in, I didn't hear Mrs Skarseth come, I don't know how long...'

He does not say all this, he does not say any of it. Perhaps I am thinking, what a callous soul, this Johanna! Is there a hope in the prison cell that she will abandon her callousness? No, for in the next instant we know clearly that this additional revenge has become dearer to her than her first desperate impulse. Not only has she hated and killed Sonja, that angel of God, she has struck her twice over by letting her lover be dragged into the course of events: a gift from — well, from the gods. As for herself, she would willingly have accepted her punishment; she had not thought as far as that. When the gods sent her this scapegoat, yes this damned goat who had glorified the 'innocent' Sonja's lamb-like life, then the gods gave meaning to the brief joy of revenge, to something which otherwise had no meaning in the long run. A callous soul? A soul in need, who in an instant hardened herself to an incredible degree. All that happiness of which her life had been a caricature now lay flat, dead, a grimace; as her own life had been a caricature, a grimace — a counterfeit echo of a dream of freedom. Such harsh conditions prevail in that slough we make of our lives. It is called No Man's Land, and has no frontiers across which to flee...

He does not reply. His silence is the equivalent of an admission of guilt, almost the equivalent. They have asked him repeatedly, but he keeps silent. He intends to make it difficult. No regret, write the papers.

And as for the motive — ! No need to go far to look for that. Naturally the young woman would not submit to his demands, it's as simple as that; public opinion believes it's as simple as that. An ageing old goat like that, is what public opinion believes. Sentenced previously for something or other. Besides, these men who are used to getting their own way — ! Man's animal lust. Man's bestial rage when he is denied his imaginary rights. Oh yes, the motive is as clear as daylight. We know these men; they ought to be hanged, whipped — a continual danger to public safety.

On the other hand no deliberate intent, let alone premeditation. No real desire to kill, rather assault and battery perhaps, with death to...

Six years. Why not six? Half twelve, twice three. The middle of the tree, the tree of justice. The defendant acquiesced in the sentence.

We acquiesced in the sentence, did we not? Six years are a continuation too. And Sonja is dead: a sacrifice to an assumption, *his* assumption. He had, after all, guessed that Johanna was vindictive; he had even suspected the matter of the inheritance from the very first: that Mrs Skarseth might be expected to squander a certain inheritance, in addition to all the concern that rankled most at her daughter's heart. She covered Sonja with the blanket, didn't she? She kissed Sonja good night.

And he himself has said that time does not exist. So he must have *wanted* it to happen — once he had come to grief. He has everything to lose.

    We acquiesced in the sentence. I in the House acquiesced in it. I have acquiesced in things for a long time now.

    ...against my will, against my will, against my will!

19

An autumn day, a morning like any other. Perhaps a little brighter after welcome rain. A little more brilliant to unaccustomed eyes. The trees in the park with the bronze child — their crowns are still green, with a dash of yellow here and there, transitory gold.

His movements are slow, almost unsteady. Perhaps because he is unused to looking at such great distances; and then all this freedom of choice.

It may also be because he has no objective. He's just drifting. He's without any objective because he's ignorant of it, yet he has it in him without knowing it, or at any rate without wishing to know. That's probably why he's wandering in the park, shuttling backwards and forwards in a strange way between the hotel and the post office, though it's not exactly the post office — it looks as if it's the building next door. There used to be a public hall there, a place for speakers to influence public opinion and all that kind of thing. It's been turned into a cinema now, with gaudy posters of ladies with magnificent busts. Maybe they influence public opinion as well.

And while he shuttles between these two outer points, long pauses in front of the bronze child, as if he's investigating it. Afterwards he walks slowly along the straight street out towards the railway station and puts his small knapsack into the left luggage office. So he's not going to travel? He had a motor cycle once, didn't he, but that's not on his mind, neither that nor a child's windblown garment on the back of a chair. All that is out of his thoughts. As he walks along the straight road back from the station it almost seems as if he's getting wind of his way forward, like a dog, yes, like an absent-minded dog who takes a good sniff from time to time, but in between forgets its purpose completely, if it ever had one.

But then he reappears in the same streets again and again, as if he were encircling the house in ever-decreasing laps. Suddenly he's there, on the other side of the street, looking up at the windows on the second floor.

No flower pots there any more, no starched curtains which seemed to draw themselves back dramatically to display their tableau of pots and decorative objects. Now a few thin strips of curtain hang straight down with empty window sills between them. It might be accommodating an evening school.

He crosses the street quickly and mounts the stairs two by two. It doesn't make him out of breath; he doesn't need to pause, feeling dizzy before he rings the bell. All the same, his heart starts hammering as soon as he hears footsteps in the passage inside. It is still hammering when the reply comes. 'Mrs Skarseth? Guest house?' A shake of the head. He goes down, taking the stairs singly. Relieved? He had not hoped for anything. And if he had not met a man at the entrance who had *Caretaker* written all over him and was simply begging to be asked, he would have walked past him. But the man almost barred his way with his evident need to communicate. And he has a ready answer. He knows very well where Mrs Skarseth lives, Mrs Skarseth poor thing, as he expresses himself: crazy about those refugees of hers, but then she suffered for it in the end. And thank heaven for the daughter who arrived back in town just at the time when one of the refugees raped and murdered the kind girl who lived there. Devoted ladies, those teachers. Together they had bought a little house on the edge of town, and the daughter ran some kind of school, and they kept chickens, well he doesn't know, but that's what he's heard. He can in addition say exactly in which direction the house is to be found. But it's far. It's not worth walking.

So he walks. It is far. But the caretaker was mistaken. It is worth walking. It's true, it wasn't worth it as long as he was only wandering about. Now it's slightly worth it; it seems to make him feel freer. He thinks the word and is about to smile. But he is unused to smiling; the correct muscles are out of training. So the smile inside him results in a tiny little grimace around the mouth. He is very cautious about his behaviour as he walks. It's not wise to be watched when one has such thoughts.

To the right after the yellow newsstand, said the caretaker. The first turning after the newsstand, the fourth or fifth house on the left. His pace slows suddenly. And his heart starts hammering once more. For he has no purpose in connection with his visit, even less than when he went to the guesthouse. For now that he knows where it is he hopes for absolutely nothing.

He walks past the fourth house, glances about him, looks over the low picket fence. No chickens. Besides, the house is red not brown. He pauses. A young girl is coming from the same direction, overtaking him when he stops, a cheerful girl of about sixteen. She asks him politely whether he is looking for any particular house. He thanks her and says no. Not for anything in particular. She gives him a friendly nod and goes in through a gate. Behind the trees, almost hidden, is a house. It is brown, an old timber house. Now he can hear the cackle of chickens. A little further along the fence he can see an open yard with a water pump in the middle. An old woman is sitting on a bench in front of it. She lifts her head. What a remarkably vital head on such an aged body! Yes, she is raising her head towards the young girl, who drops her school bag to the ground, pauses for a second, then runs forward and throws her arms round the old woman's neck. The old woman has risen to her feet. Now she holds out her arms, they are Mrs Skarseth's arms, her way of holding them out. Once she had told him that she had held out her arms like that to a daughter who had returned home. Now it is a granddaughter who is embracing her!

He stands, deeply moved, watching. Quick questions and answers between the two of them, about school and chickens, about Mother, about when she's coming home. He cannot distinguish every word, because there is such a loud ringing sound in his ears. His whole being is ringing and singing. Somewhere a flood of tears is hidden. They have been mounting up behind a dam that became thicker and more solid with every day that passed, and which became thinner and weaker with every night. One white hen comes out into the yard. But he watches it through tears: it turns into many hens, a little crooked, a little deformed. And when he leaves, distancing himself more and more quickly with each step, everything becomes deformed: houses, trees and flowing fences, heaving like the sea. A simple brick house with a yellow gable tips up and moves towards him. He shields himself with his hands and bends over; he falls under this gable which is trying to crush him. But it does not crush him. It stands there. He gets up again, and now he runs alongside the heaving fences. When he reaches the newsstand he stops suddenly and gives himself a few brief words of command. The newsagent sticks out his head and asks what he wants. He buys a newspaper and notes the date. Four years. Six years had been commuted to four. His behaviour had been exemplary.

So what now? He remains standing. The newsagent looks up from his magazine, probably thinking he's an odd person. For the first time during all this he is thinking for himself. He thinks, the newsagent must think I'm an odd person. So he begins walking again. But this time in the opposite manner: first quickly, then slowly, and gradually so slowly that he is almost not walking at all. What had the caretaker said? It's not worth walking.

No. It's not worth it. He thinks confusedly, what is worth it? A short while ago he was hurrying forward; now he is almost standing still. Shortly before that again he was walking with firm steps in the opposite direction, the one it was not worth taking.

Was it worth it?

He asks without embarrassment straight out into the sunshine whether it was worth it. And again somebody turns with an astonished expression. It must be good to get away from here. To get away. To reach a frontier. It must be good.

There is no frontier.

That is the next thought he stops to consider. And now he repeats it aloud. He knows with sudden unmistakable certainty: there is no frontier. Has he always known? That time in the big house, or when they took his papers away?... No, no, nobody took them; they blew away in the wind. That's how it was. That had happened just beside a frontier. He had believed so.

And yet he stands here, telling the dark sunshine that there is no frontier. He means something specific: in our own minds there are no

frontiers, no limits to our suffering.
He is speaking again. Atonement is impossible, he says.

I can reach him now. I have never let him go. Now I seem to be reaching him more and more. I hum to him under my breath that the possibility of happiness has been created for these Skarseths, for the 'guilty' persons. He laughs it away, or rather, he smiles his ugly grimace. That means he rejects all illusions. He is now sixty years old, says this grimace, erect, grey-haired, empty and almost without a past. Free. Free — !

How that grimace is unbecoming to him! Its intention is to say: the past is always, always in the future. I tell him that actions lead to all evil. He replies with Sonja's words: so should I simply sit with my hands in my lap? And I answer him again with his own words: why not? It's a good thing to do with your hands. Then he looks at his two hands, lifting them up like two strange objects and contemplating them. Some words pass through his mind about everything two such hands have been used for, everything they have held — who said that? Then he notices a stripe on each of his wrists, as if made by hard, narrow bands. The English chair, he thinks. But they do not pain him any more, his wrists, and that was many lives ago, after all. These stigmata, he thinks, in the mind — and in the flesh. They exist and continue to exist. There is no frontier.

Then afterwards he walks. It is good to walk. It is better than the alternative, not to walk. He walks to the town, and straight across the town. He does not call in at the railway station to fetch his knapsack. He walks straight through the town and out into the country on the other side. The sun is already setting, all the shadows are lengthening and turning a deeper grey. Then there are no shadows, the sky turns dark, a sudden shower of rain is falling. Afterwards it becomes lighter again before night falls. He passes a garage, a small café beside it, about to close. He'd rather not go in; he'd prefer to sit on the step and eat. They allow him to do so. He has the money he earned during the four years. They stare at him, a little surprised, when he asks their permission. He can sit inside if he likes: people may sit inside when it is clear they have money. But he does not wish to sit inside, not anywhere, not inside.

He wishes to walk. Perhaps he will rest for a little at the edge of the forest. In the grey morning light he is still walking. He passes a little house behind a lawn behind a fence. No chair is standing on the lawn, no little blue garment is hanging on it, without sleeves. Words form themselves in him: has he served his time for this guilt? But the words are succeeded by an ugly grimace, which expresses scorn, which contradicts him, which says: I have not asked for freedom.

It says: You *can* serve your sentence, but you are not freed by it; you do not become a child again. You can only walk on. That's the only thing you can do. But you cannot arrive anywhere. There is no frontier.

20

He's coming!
Are the heavy fir trees sighing a warning? Are the birches murmuring in the wind?

I am chasing away mere phantoms, this morning as so many mornings. Many old friends are knocking on your door and brooding out in the dark night. Peter Gustov — you remembered him every single night in the cell; he came and offered his services: his arts as a host, his invitation to eternal hopelessness. The sanguine general, Old Buster, without responsibility, without any other pleasure than failed hopes. The peevish taskmaster Mr Financier — we had always known him in his melancholy insatiability, his irony. The self-loving couple in their deathly stagnation and meaningless beauty. Only one of them was alive: Daniel, the Auxiliary. He was evil. He hated his conscience, his Oliver. Any why is goodness always weak?

Why are you yourself so weak now that you're on your way? I watch you pass the house by the road with bent head. No garment is hanging over the chair; there is no chair. Be bold now, look up, look everything in the eye!

But he bends his head. Why is your courage always weak? You have the courage to come, after all. You are not coming, you say; not coming *to*, only *from*? Always in flight, in other words? Your shoes are slipping off your feet; they were not made for such a long journey. Well — you know that, I expect. You made them yourself during those long years. You made a thousand or more such pairs of shoes; they were made for short walks, for walks where each step did not burn as if treading on a hot iron.

But you're coming! I'm keeping the air fresh for you, ridding it of these shadows that you yourself have created. Perhaps they will flee for good one day? Oh, you don't believe so? We'll agree on that, then. You know best. For you yourself have said that there is no frontier, there is no place or stage on our way that we can cross with any finality, and say, now it's over and done with.

Isn't there? You don't even believe in death, I suppose. You'll find that you, the sceptic, believe in eternal life, not in hope, but in fear. And if it is so — well, well, well, at least you're turning your back on your aimless activities, on your way towards an objective, in order to rest in an identity which is certainly your own, even though it's also a hard path to tread, even though what ought to be proved as well is that nothing ever ends.

At any rate I'm chasing these guests away. At least you have the right to that. They take their time about it. The bartender, for instance, goes on repeating his eternal refrain about immutability and echoes.

But if everything is an echo, a distorted and loathsome echo, perhaps the original sound was less beautiful than you thought at first! Your ego was perhaps not worth the repetition, not worth the caricatured reproduction which is called life. All right, but in that case don't blame the repetition! An echo has no power in itself; it merely multiplies the truth.

And I *can* hear you're coming. That is what the fir trees are booming, the birches murmuring. Of course he's coming, whispers the fishing net by the lake, just above the fragile jetty. A robin redbreast got caught there once; you freed it and felt it as a good deed in your hands. Such hands. They have held so much, for good and evil.

And you believed something, or hoped or imagined or — I don't know; that time you stood by the fence and wept behind a tree, and felt for a second that you had created a situation that was worth the sacrifice. Where did those tears come from otherwise? And perhaps I am wrong to say that your last attack on a world of action was only in vain, or even worse: a fatal challenge to someone who had paused in his flight. Perhaps I was mistaken, and this, too, had to happen; had to happen in order to cleanse the impurities out of a personality which had merely mirrored itself for far too long. That time you stood on the crest of the hill — is it four years ago? It was spring then, now it's autumn, and perhaps there was only a summer in between — but that day: what if you had turned back? You were tempted by a squirrel. Everything tempted you. You did not turn back. Perhaps you won? No, not the world. One does not win the world. One loses one's soul; but one does not win the world. Perhaps you won your soul back? No, no, I'll not use big words. Perhaps you won back an inch of that identity you had squandered so thoroughly.

In that case I have not been chasing phantoms away in vain. Don't call it a victory. Don't believe you'll reach any goal. Call it a cessation of flight. We have fallen silent on the way. Soon you will be standing on the crest of the rise again. Then we shall know. Look at the lake, how it's waiting! Its surface is slate-grey now. But a mere ripple of the wind, and it plays in colours you knew once, before it turned grey.

Yes, it's autumn. Not a bad time of year. Maybe it doesn't promise so very much in our forest. The cell had green walls. Here there are many yellow leaves. Soon there will be rime in the fishing net by the jetty, as in your own hair. Soon it will be cold. We don't object to that so much any longer, even though it will be very cold. There's something cleansing about it. Everything here is wondering about one thing: whether he's coming, whether he'll dare to stand by his convictions.

He's on his way. The birds have seen him; they're swaying on the branches, twittering. Over there a fish surfaced, causing a play of colour in the water, that's all it takes. It's as if everything is carrying a message: he's bound to come.

But it's still a long way. The shoes which were so handsome are slipping off his feet. So he takes them off. They're no use any longer. It's not worth walking, said the caretaker. His bare feet are being burnt by the road — on fire. It's a little cooler when he turns on to the path. In some places you can walk on the grass, but there are plenty of treacherous twigs and stones. He feels them less and less. His feet are burning up to and above his ankles. His head is burning too; there are flames in front of his eyes, which were used to green walls. He has been walking for two days and a night. What can a caretaker like that mean by saying it's not worth it? Does the man know something special?

At the Farm an old man comes out. 'You've been gone a long time,' he says. 'You've been gone all the summer.' He's so old he doesn't know the difference between a summer and four years. He no longer lives on this earth; he knows nothing. But he has strange eyes, searching eyes. 'A very long time,' he says. But his voice is kind and gentle, a little wheezy with age. He has not read a newspaper for twenty five years. He knows nothing, nothing at all. He just exists.

You nod and walk past, neither confirming nor denying that anything has been a long time. You look, like him, up into the sky, at the weather. It's an old custom, a matter of courtesy. You're on your way the whole time. And after the farm the path narrows and almost disappears. Often it cannot be seen, for it is dusk at the base of the green sea of grass. Light lies on the hilltops, sprawling blotches of light. At one spot a pine tree stands, as red — yes, as red as blood. The path climbs up hill and down dale, not roundabout, but just as somebody made it in his simplicity in the dawn of time.

Of course, he thinks, in the dawn of time. It is the evening of time now. All one has to do is simply walk. But it's not a matter of 'simply', for he is dizzied by inner light in the darkness. And up on the hilltops, where it really is light, the sun has turned black, everything has turned black. He stumbles and gets to his feet; he stumbles again and lies there briefly. It's good to lie for a little before you get up again and walk. Getting up isn't so easy. All right, so you can crawl. You can crawl on hands and knees. After a while his hands start bleeding as well, like his feet. They're not accustomed to being used for walking.

He's coming!

Can you see him? Can *you* see him? Grasses nod, grasses sway and ask. Fir trees are whispering gently. Soon it will be restful here. Yes, he's coming. He's coming up the last slope, the one that leads to the top. So now what? He's getting to his feet up there! I see myself standing in the halo of sun. I am standing beside the wall of the house in the smell of paint and sun-warmed timber. I retreat to the edge of the forest. The last ray of sun is falling on the fishing net beside the

jetty, glimmering like burnished copper. Beneath it lies the boat in shadow, slowly and patiently rocking to and fro on its rope.
But the sun is still up there. It spins its gold about him. Will he turn? I say softly, but loudly enough so that it is said:
'If he turns back now he is lost.'
He does not turn back. He's coming!
He walks up the slopes on his feet. For a moment it looks as if he's going to kneel. But no, he's walking. Not fast, but he's walking. At the foot of the slope he falls, gets up once, and falls again.
Are there shadows in the air? I chased them away so firmly. No, no shadows. Sonja is here: she's no shadow, she *exists*. Victory is not important. What is important, then? Now it is important to arrive, my friend, to join — me.
So he does not get up. His hands are caked with blood now; they are useless. So he crawls on elbows and knees the last stretch of the way. And that is from where the slope ends, and up to the house. It is red and grey; red as blood, grey as a grey day: a good house to be in for someone who is on the way to himself and knows that there are no frontiers to cross.
So he crawls on elbows and knees. Then he creeps. But his head is held high.
Then that, too, droops. His head is no longer held high.
I walk forward from my edge of the forest. We are one before we meet. He is I. He reaches the house. Now he is beside the steps, the steps of my house in the forest, from which no plans will emerge, no roads reach out to strive for frontiers.
So I arrive at the steps and rest my head against the threshold.